# Books as Partners

# Books as Partners

## *Diverse Literature in the Early Childhood Classroom*

Lesley Colabucci
Mary Napoli

ROWMAN & LITTLEFIELD
Lanham • Boulder • New York • London

Published by Rowman & Littlefield
An imprint of The Rowman & Littlefield Publishing Group, Inc.
4501 Forbes Boulevard, Suite 200, Lanham, Maryland 20706
www.rowman.com

6 Tinworth Street, London SE11 5AL, United Kingdom

Copyright © 2020 by Lesley Colabucci and Mary Napoli

*All rights reserved.* No part of this book may be reproduced in any form or by any electronic or mechanical means, including information storage and retrieval systems, without written permission from the publisher, except by a reviewer who may quote passages in a review.

British Library Cataloguing in Publication Information Available

**Library of Congress Cataloging-in-Publication Data**

Names: Colabucci, Lesley, 1970– author. | Napoli, Mary, author.
Title: Books as partners : diverse literature in the early childhood classroom / Lesley Colabucci, Mary Napoli.
Description: Lanham : Rowman & Littlefield, [2020] | Includes bibliographical references and index. | Summary: "Books as Partners is designed to assist teachers in integrating high quality diverse literature to support instruction across the curriculum"— Provided by publisher.
Identifiers: LCCN 2020012596 (print) | LCCN 2020012597 (ebook) | ISBN 9781475847352 (cloth) | ISBN 9781475847369 (paperback) | ISBN 9781475847376 (epub)
Subjects: LCSH: Literature—Study and teaching (Early childhood)—United States. | Children's literature—Study and teaching (Early childhood)—United States. | Children—Books and reading. | Cultural awareness—Study and teaching (Early childhood)—United States. | Multicultural education—United States.
Classification: LCC LB1139.5.L58 C65 2020 (print) | LCC LB1139.5.L58 (ebook) | DDC 372.64/044—dc23
LC record available at https://lccn.loc.gov/2020012596
LC ebook record available at https://lccn.loc.gov/2020012597

To Dr. Rudine Sims Bishop,
whose groundbreaking and enduring work in
children's literature paved the way for this book

# Contents

| | | |
|---|---|---|
| Acknowledgments | | ix |
| Introduction | | xi |
| 1 | Partnering with the Self: Affirming and Understanding Identity | 1 |
| 2 | Partnering at Home: Knowing Your Family | 19 |
| 3 | Partnering at School: Being Friends | 43 |
| 4 | Partnering Within the Community: Nurturing a Sense of Belonging | 59 |
| 5 | Partnering Globally: Understanding the World | 79 |
| Appendix: Resources to Locate Diverse Selections | | 99 |
| Index | | 101 |
| About the Authors | | 107 |

# Acknowledgments

*Books as Partners* was only made possible through the inspiration, assistance, and support of our colleagues, families, friends, and students. We relied heavily on the Lancaster Public Library, McNairy Library at Millersville University, and the Penn State Harrisburg Library for resources of all sorts (including workspace). As always, librarians were there to save the day. We are grateful to the publishers who were willing to share books with us along the way and in helping to coordinate the author interviews. Thank you to the authors/illustrators for taking the time to answer our questions and for sharing your talents with readers of all ages: Janet Wong, Leslea Newman, Derrick Barnes, Matt de la Peña, and Duncan Tonatiuh.

We would also like to extend our sincere appreciation to the teachers whose classroom stories are showcased in this book. Thank you, Sarah Hamill and Veronica O'Leary, for sharing high-quality literature with your students to transform readers "one book at a time."

At Millersville University, Lesley received support in the form of a sabbatical leave. She would like to thank Ruth Salinkas and Kelly Davis for their encouragement and random printing favors. Her family, Barb Smentek and Andre Colabucci, provided endless support and patience. Her father, Lawrence Colabucci, was a teacher and principal and a role model for her as an educator.

At Penn State Harrisburg, Mary received the support and encouragement to complete this project from her school director, Dr. Mark Kiselica. She would also like to acknowledge the Penn State Harrisburg library faculty and staff for their assistance and support. Moreover, she would like to thank her parents, Josephine and Patrick, for their unwavering support throughout this endeavor. Her sister, Victoria, also provided endless notes of encouragement.

Lastly, she would like to thank Lesley Colabucci for co-authoring this book and for sharing her knowledge and passion for children's literature.

Finally, we would like to thank Rowman & Littlefield for bringing our vision to fruition.

# Introduction

Is it necessary to infuse diverse literature in the early childhood classroom? Why, and for what purpose? How can diverse literature be woven throughout the early childhood curriculum? Diverse literature plays an increasingly significant role in the early childhood classroom, especially as communities become more global and diverse. In today's early childhood classrooms, educators are faced with increasing demands to match curricular standards to the developmental needs of their learners. The overarching goal of *Books as Partners* is to assist teachers in integrating high-quality diverse literature to support instruction across the curriculum. Throughout the book, readers will find guidelines for selecting high-quality literature that contains rich language, authentic voices, and text that is free of stereotypes and misrepresentations.

This book is designed to serve as a tool to help early childhood educators develop children's understanding of their cultural communities as well as foster cross-cultural understandings. By including diverse literature in the early childhood classroom, teachers can facilitate and co-construct dialogue about differences, diversity, and respect. When young readers are exposed to diverse children's literature, they are provided with opportunities to explore their backgrounds and values and well as learn about the people living in their community and beyond. Through the application of multimodal text sets, or collections of connected books and resources, young children and their teachers will develop new understandings and respect for others. Considering the power that books hold for children of all cultures, teachers have a responsibility to select high-quality books with positive and authentic themes that will facilitate identity development while promoting acceptance and understanding of others.

In order to become culturally competent citizens who value and respect others, every young child must have opportunities to learn about and understand the lives and views of people whose race, ethnicity, nationality, religion, family structure, immigration status, abilities, gender, and sexual orientation differ from their own. Carefully selected, developmentally appropriate, and culturally accurate diverse literature can provide young children with access to authentic voices that communicate a wide range of emotions, attitudes, and experiences beyond those that are familiar to them. Diverse books, when organized in text sets and linked across the curriculum, can open windows into aspects of the world in order to build empathy toward others while supporting interdisciplinary instruction.

Teachers are often drawn to books that offer simple and direct themes related to topics such as anti-bullying, kindness, and making friends. These are important issues to address in the early childhood classroom, but as Turner (2019), a first-grade teacher, has found, the ways kindness is taught in early childhood classrooms can be problematic. He argues that when we talk about kindness without addressing justice, we are negating children's experiences. He has taught his students not just about the ideas of bias or stereotypes but also about microaggressions. This has enabled his students to see where unkindness might come from and how to deal with it more directly and justly. He emphasizes that "moving away from simple kindness and toward real justice begins with building an identity-safe classroom: a place where everyone's story is not only recognized but honored, studied and loved" (unpaged). Talking about our differences doesn't divide us or estrange us from one another; instead it offers an opportunity to come together in a more authentic, inclusive, and respectful way.

A concerted effort must be made by new and experienced classroom teachers to employ a critical lens as they face the challenge of finding quality books that honestly portray the complexities of diversity while also reflecting the demographics of their classroom and the world. Diverse children's literature should include representations of different aspects of daily life within a culture, with particular attention given to aspects of setting and racial relevance (Yenika-Agbaw & Napoli, 2011). Readers of all ages deserve to have access to exemplary books that feature characters similar to themselves and communities like theirs. In addition, all children need books that broaden their perspectives by accurately and authentically presenting different voices. The multimodal text sets presented throughout the book present one way to connect children to interesting stories, enhance the curriculum, and explore social justice perspectives. By recommending multimodal text sets for classrooms and literary spaces, we offer one way to raise the standard for quality and sophistication in the kinds of stories we share with young children.

Multimodal text sets provide educators with purposeful and literacy-rich ways to infuse literature selections from various genres to support the varied paths to cognitive and literacy development of young children. *Multimodal* refers to a combination of print, visual images, video clips, hyperlinks, audio clips, and other modes of representation (Kress & van Leeuwen, 1996; Jewitt, 2008; Kress, 2010; Serafini, 2012, 2015). Reading high-quality diverse literature on a regular basis with students also aligns with the National Association for the Education of Young Children's (NAEYC) Early Childhood Program Standards and Accreditation Criteria (2012) and early literacy skills (e.g., print motivation, narrative skills/comprehension, vocabulary, etc.). The NAEYC's main agenda of equipping teachers in early childhood programs with the tools to treat all children with respect and consideration remains at the heart of *Books as Partners*. While diverse literature is one component of culturally responsive pedagogy, it is critical that teachers be able to select books that not only foster a deep appreciation of reading but also allow students to see themselves in the world. Culturally responsive teaching seeks to respect the humanity of every person, prioritizing teachers' and children's personal, practical knowledge as foundational to promoting change in early childhood settings and beyond (Souto-Manning, 2013). Diverse multimodal text sets, when incorporated in the classroom, can make a difference in breaking barriers, dispelling stereotypes, and fostering cultural competence.

The demographics of the United States are shifting at a growing rate; the U.S. Census Bureau (2015) estimates that by the year 2042, groups currently categorized as racial minorities will account for a majority of the U.S. population. This national call translates to a need for early childhood educators to provide their students with the tools to successfully navigate the world beyond the classroom, and incorporating diverse literature is one vehicle to begin building the foundations for cultural competence. Cultural competence is a multilayered set of skills that enable effective interactions with people from other cultures. Diverse text sets will offer young readers opportunities to build their understanding of differences and the diversity within their community and their world. As scholar Richard Beach (2005) discovered, "In responding to literature, students are experiencing characters' complex, often inexplicable reactions to these events that defy rational explanations" (p. 7); the experience that students have can actually transform into a process of building cultural competence through the quality of their responses to the materials. Through exemplary selections of culturally authentic, accurate, and diverse literature that move children beyond the story, literacy experience in the early childhood classroom can facilitate both identity development and cultural competence.

## THE IMPORTANCE OF MIRRORS

There is ample evidence that there is a lack of diversity in children's literature (Bishop, 1990, 2012; McNair, 2008, 2014; Horning, Lindgren, & Schliesman, 2013; Thomas, 2016). Based on documentation from the Cooperative Children's Book Center (CCBC; ccbc.education.wisc.edu), children's literature continues to be dominated by portrayals of white, middle-class culture. These portrayals are not consistent with the children and their respective families with whom teachers work every day in early childhood classrooms. Gay (2000) argues that the curriculum for culturally diverse students must be inclusive and portray their realities. An authentic multicultural curriculum not only reflects a range of diversity but also has the capacity to empower readers to consider larger issues of social justice. With the increased instructional demands within the early childhood setting, teachers can incorporate diverse text sets to meet national standards, ensure that selections are authentic and developmentally appropriate, and provide engaging literature responses across the curriculum.

The argument for books as "mirrors and windows" sets the foundation for the inclusion of diverse books in the classroom. As Thomas (2017) states, "Here is an uncomfortable truth: in children's and young adult literature, Whiteness has long been the dominant narrative perspective" (unpaged). The effects of this enduring disparity are hard to quantify, but the child's self-concept and well-being are at risk if teachers fail to deliberately and meaningfully incorporate diverse books. Despite the increased diversity in children's books as well as in other media and materials such as toys, white children are still dramatically more likely to see themselves in these materials than children from other backgrounds. The Cooperative Children's Book Center, #weneeddiversebooks, and specialized publishers such as Lee & Low continue to collect data on diversity in children's publishing. These reports indicate slow progress with recent (2018) statistics showing approximately 73 percent of books published still feature white characters. As shown in figure I.1, the percentage of books with representations of people of color continues to be dismal.

It is important to note that the data represented in the infographic include titles that offer children the opportunity to see themselves pictorially, but without any direct content related to racial or cultural markers or meaning. These statistics also do not account for the negative and inaccurate portrayals that are found across children's media. The infographic attempts to show this by including "cracks in the mirrors to illustrate the continued misrepresentation of the underrepresented communities—the quantity of books may have gone up, but it isn't all good news as that doesn't necessarily indicate accuracy and quality in the titles" (SLJ staff, 2019, para. 4). The harm done by long-term exposure to the kind of imagery found in racist or otherwise biased

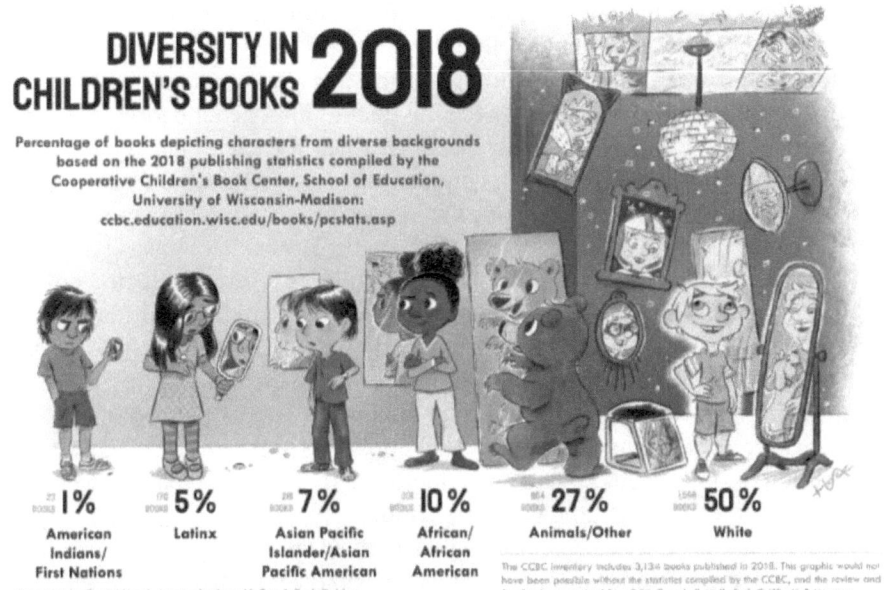

Diversity in Children's Books 2018. *Source: Huyck, D., & S. P. Dahlen. (2019, June 19). Diversity in children's books 2018. sarahpark.com blog. Created in consultation with Edith Campbell, Molly Beth Griffin, K. T. Horning, Debbie Reese, Ebony Elizabeth Thomas, and Madeline Tyner, with statistics compiled by the Cooperative Children's Book Center, School of Education, University of Wisconsin-Madison: ccbc.education.wisc.edu/books/pcstats.asp. Retrieved from readingspark.wordpress.com/2019/06/19/picture-this-diversity-in-childrens-books-2018-infographic*

books serves as an additional call to action to integrate diverse books in the early childhood classroom. In order to combat this harm and promote the best diverse books, each chapter of *Books as Partners* empowers teachers to take action and transform their classrooms and instructional practices.

## ORGANIZATION AND STRUCTURE

The book is divided into five content or topical chapters. Each chapter features an overarching theme aligned with an important subject addressed in early childhood classrooms. These topics were selected based on NAEYC curriculum guidelines and standards. They reflect the research on young children's development and social worlds as well as the realities of interactions in preschool and early childhood classrooms.

In each chapter, the authors have organized several "text sets" for consideration. These clusters of books were carefully curated with an emphasis on recent titles, trends in children's literature, literary quality, and availability. Literary genre was limited to realistic fiction and picture books with a few exceptions for simple nonfiction titles that could also be categorized as beginner books. As we searched for and read titles for each chapter, we also ensured that the books reflected the highest standards for multicultural literature. The best books from each compilation are then featured in the text sets. The titles for each set emerged through an analysis process that was based on reviews and further research into each book. Searches were conducted online as well as at the library. Various databases were utilized as well as review sources, and each book was vetted for literary quality and anti-bias. Another goal was to include books from a range of publishers and ones that are readily available through public library holdings. Overly popular books or classics were not included since the intention was to present as many new books as possible. Books were only included if they received positive reviews and would be engaging to young children.

Each book in a text set is annotated with ideas for classroom use and multimodal connections. In order to further demonstrate the appeal and potential of these books, classroom vignettes were collected. These classroom stories are shared to capture the ways teachers and children might utilize and respond to the books. Finally, each chapter concludes with words from one of the authors of a book featured in the text set. The authors were selected for a variety of reasons, including the appeal of their book from the text set and their role as an expert or trailblazer in multicultural children's literature.

Chapter 1 focuses on the concept of physical attributes with an emphasis on self-love. The book choices for this chapter were driven by the need to promote awareness, acceptance, and confidence. Ample research shows that very young children notice and are trying to make sense of racial, ethnic, and other kinds of differences (Winkler, 2009). While evidence shows that most white parents avoid talking about race, parents of children of color are much more likely to address differences and matters of race with their children. White children need to feel comfortable talking about differences they notice and perhaps do not understand, while children of color need affirmation in order to counter the negative messages within society. In Kutner's (1993) reporting on Katz's groundbreaking 1973 study, he concludes that "one of the most important things parents can do to help children appreciate people who are different than they are is to make diversity a topic of conversation from an early age" (p. 12). Chapter 1 provides caregivers and educators with a range of resources to facilitate that conversation.

In chapter 2, the focus switches from individual identity markers to the broader context of families. Integrating families is a key component of quality early childhood education. Teachers already understand the importance of providing a supportive and inclusive space for their students and their families. Children from families that are outside of the traditional image of a mom and dad with a biological child need to see themselves reflected in stories and other materials. The goal for this chapter was to feature a wide range of family types and to seek balance in terms of other demographics.

The books selected include LGBTQ families, single-parent families, divorced families, interracial families, adoptive families, and families in transitions. These particular types of families were selected based on demographic research utilizing the census website as well as what was currently published and available. The books were examined, and then text sets were developed not based on family types but on the overarching themes across the books. Thus, the books are organized around commonalities and intersectionalities that acknowledge the multiple ways family types may overlap. This chapter also includes some books that are collections, rather than stories, and portray multiple kinds of families. Overall, these recommended books can be infused to celebrate a range of families even if none are present in the classroom.

Chapter 3 addresses the typical experiences that children encounter at school. A particular focus has been made to explore issues of diversity that are in play as children negotiate social interactions related to making friends and interacting with their peers. The books selected aim to help children address fears about the first day of school, learn to take risks in social contexts, and make new friends across lines of difference. As children struggle more and more with social anxiety and with the increased need for bullying prevention, these books are especially important. Teachers, parents, and other stakeholders must recognize the ways schools reinforce various biases and exclusionary practices. The text sets delve into the complicated ways differences play out in children's social worlds.

Chapter 4 explores the role of the broader community in children's lives. Children navigate social worlds inside and outside of school and family. Their neighborhoods and towns fulfill an aspect of their identity and shape their experiences. Early childhood educators often teach about community by focusing on neighborhood helpers and other positive attributes. The books in this chapter celebrate all kinds of neighborhoods and address issues such as poverty and housing insecurity. These books also celebrate different kinds of friendships, such as those with grandparents or other older members of the community. This chapter functions as an invitation to teachers to embrace all members of the communities in which they teach.

Chapter 5 reaches beyond the local context to consider the global community. Children's books with a global perspective offer children insight into the world beyond their borders and life experience. These books are increasingly available due to the current political context, and many classrooms have an increased population of immigrant and refugee children. While immigration is not a new topic in children's books, the collection developed here only features contemporary stories with an emphasis on relocation and border crossings. The books in this text set are organized around themes such as times of crisis and making connections; they feature a range of countries and capture the ways traditions transcend place. Teachers will find these books honest and realistic in their portrayals, hopefully resonating with children who are experiencing transitions.

## CONCLUSION

As early childhood educators begin thinking more about how to infuse multimodal text sets related to diverse topics, they will generate more student-centered examples and engagements to share with colleagues, families, and administrators. By infusing the recommended literature selections within the curriculum and by providing a collective space for dialogue, teachers are taking the necessary steps to foster a strong sense of self-worth in all children. Finally, educators should review their current classroom library to ensure the inclusion of diverse and culturally relevant selections across genres. Quality books as mirrors are needed to ensure that their students see themselves in the literature and in the classroom. Teachers can also reach out to school or public librarians for assistance in evaluating their classroom selections and for book recommendations. There is an online survey tool available at Lee & Low Books' website (www.leeandlow.com/educators/grade-level-resources/classroom-library-questionnaire) that teachers can use individually or collectively within their professional learning communities. Teachers can also refer to award lists that celebrate diverse books that provide further conversation and insights, such as the Pura Belpré and Coretta Scott King, among others (see the appendix).

## REFERENCES

Beach, R. (2005). Conducting research on teaching literature: The influence of texts, contexts, and teacher on responses to multicultural literature. Paper presented at the National Reading Conference, Miami, FL.

Bishop, R. S. (1990). Mirrors, windows and sliding glass doors. *Perspectives, 6*(3), ix–xi.

Bishop, R. S. (2012). Reflections on the development of African American children's literature. *Journal of Children's Literature, 38*(2), 5–13.

Gay, G. (2000). *Culturally responsive teaching: Theory, research, and practice*. New York, NY: Teachers College Press.

Horning, K. T., Lindgren, M. V., & Schliesman, M. (2013). A few observations on publishing in 2012. *CCBC Choices 2013*. Retrieved from https://ccbc.education.wisc.edu/books/choiceintro14.asp

Huyck, D., & Dahlen, S. P. (2019, June 19). Diversity in children's books 2018. sarahpark.com blog. Created in consultation with E. Campbell, M. B. Griffin, K. T. Horning, D. Reese, E. E. Thomas, & M. Tyner, with statistics compiled by the Cooperative Children's Book Center, School of Education, University of Wisconsin-Madison: http://ccbc.education.wisc.edu/books/pcstats.asp. Retrieved from https://readingspark.wordpress.com/2019/06/19/picture-this-diversity-in-childrens-books-2018-infographic

Jewitt, C. (2008). Multimodality and literacy in the classroom. *Review of Research in Education, 32*(1), 241–267.

Katz, P. A. (1973). Perception of racial cues in preschool children: A new look. *Developmental Psychology, 8*, 295–299.

Kress, G. (2010). *Multimodality: A social semiotic approach to contemporary communication.* London, England: Routledge.

Kress, G., & van Leeuwen, T. (1996). *Reading images: The grammar of visual design.* London, England: Routledge Falmer.

Kutner, L. (1993, May 6). Parent and child. *The New York Times*, section 3, pp. 12–14.

McNair, J. C. (2008). The representation of authors and illustrators of color in school-based book clubs. *Language Arts, 85*(3), 193–201.

McNair, J. C. (2014). "I didn't know there were Black cowboys": Introducing African American families to African American children's literature. *Young Children, 69*(1), 64–69.

National Association for the Education of Young Children. (2012). Early Childhood Program Standards and Accreditation Criteria. Retrieved from www.naeyc.org

Serafini, F. (2012). Reading multimodal texts in the 21st century. *Research in the Schools, 19*(1), 26–32.

Serafini, F. (2015). Multimodal literacy: From theories to practices. *Language Arts, 92*(6), 412–423.

SLJ staff. (2019, June). An updated look at diversity in children's books. Retrieved from www.slj.com/?detailStory=an-updated-look-at-diversity-in-childrens-books

Souto-Manning, M. (2013). *Multicultural teaching in the early childhood classroom: Strategies, tools, and approaches (preschool-2nd grade).* Washington, DC: Association for Childhood Education International (ACEI); New York, NY: Teachers College Press.

Thomas, E. E. (2016). Stories still matter: Rethinking the role of diverse children's literature today. *Language Arts, 94*(2), 112–119.

Thomas, E. E. (2017, May 3). Imagine yourself a young reader in the margins, #OwnVoices: Three takes. *School Library Journal.* Retrieved from www.slj.com/?detailStory=imagine-yourself-a-young-reader-in-the-margins-ownvoices-three-takes

Turner, B. (2019). Teaching kindness isn't enough. *Teaching Tolerance, 63.* Retrieved from www.tolerance.org/magazine/fall-2019/teaching-kindness-isnt-enough?fbclid=IwAR1RwH3rAyM1aTPI2jODlBcHW4tZ-UNa1N5U_U_CZX6VCflDzJmm_NL4IW4

U.S. Census Bureau. (2015, March 3). New Census Bureau report analyzes U.S. population projections. Retrieved from www.census.gov/newsroom/press-releases/2015/cb15-tps16.html

Winkler, E. (2009). Children are not colorblind. *PACE, 3*(3), 1–8.

Yenika-Agbaw, V. S., & Napoli, M. (Eds.) (2011). *African and African American children's and adolescent literature in the classroom: A critical guide.* New York, NY: Peter Lang.

*Chapter One*

# Partnering with the Self

*Affirming and Understanding Identity*

- How can early childhood educators help students value their racial, cultural, and ethnic backgrounds while building a sense of who they are as individuals?
- What are some examples of picture books that will affirm children's identity development while also nurturing their appreciation of differences among individuals and across races and cultures?

An important part of early childhood is developing a sense of self or personal identity and exploring one's place in their world. Racial, ethnic, or cultural components are part of identity construction for young children. Ramsey (2009) explains that the development of racial identity begins early in the preschool years. At a young age, children are aware of their own racial and physical traits as well as those of the people they encounter; this awareness offers both an opportunity and a challenge for teachers. Early childhood educators play an integral role in designing a curriculum that enables young learners to develop racial and cultural pride and respect for differences. The goal of this chapter is to guide early childhood educators as they strive to affirm the diversity in their classrooms through children's books that directly address racial and cultural dimensions of identity. The featured selections invite young readers to celebrate their physical traits, respect others, and appreciate differences in their social worlds.

The chapter begins with a rationale for the need for books about self-acceptance and self-confidence related to race, culture, and ethnicity. Research on how young children reflect on their own identity markers and the importance of validating those identities through books as mirrors is emphasized, with a focus on racial features. The chapter also includes a classroom example based on a selected text, multimodal text set suggestions for classroom use, and a published children's author's perspective on the topic.

## YOUNG CHILDREN AND RACE AWARENESS

Research demonstrates that children's awareness of racial differences and the impact of racism begins quite early (Tatum, 2003; Winkler, 2009). In fact, young children are integrating racial information as part of the larger processes of socialization and education. Recent studies (Earick, 2009; Boutte et al., 2011) have shown that awareness and knowledge of race and racial differences is in play as young children negotiate their social worlds. Contrary to the idealistic notions prevalent in society, children are not colorblind. Rather than shying away from topics related to racial or cultural identity, teachers should be infusing conversations within the curriculum (Delpit, 2012; Derman-Sparks, LeeKeenan, & Nimmo, 2015). It should be reassuring to teachers that Aboud (1988, 2003) found that ethnic awareness comes before prejudice and does not relate to the formation of bias or prejudice.

Racial and cultural knowledge empowers children. By helping children establish strong positive self-concepts related to all aspects of their identities, teachers encourage them to accept both themselves and others. Children need guidance and support to reflect in meaningful ways on their identities in order to do the work of developing a positive self-concept and thus embracing themselves and their peers.

Social-emotional learning (SEL) focuses on helping children gain knowledge about feelings and getting along with others (Marion, 2011). Early childhood educators have a strong impact on their students' lives, focusing on their feelings and assisting them as they develop language for self-expression. Despite the exemplary programs supported by the NAEYC and research published to guide teachers in delivering an anti-bias curriculum (Derman-Sparks & Ramsey, 2011), there remains a need for understanding how children make sense of racial and ethnic diversity in their daily experiences.

It is important to consider how intersectionality plays a part as children negotiate and assign identities and attributes both to themselves and to others. Park's (2011) study sought to learn more about young children's understandings and actions related to racial and ethnic diversity and how these were situated in the daily life and work of a classroom community. Through a sociocultural perspective, she observed that young children actively made sense of racial and ethnic identities. For example, she directed children to draw pictures of people, providing "regular" and "skin-colored" magic markers. As students drew pictures, Park noticed their attention to detail and that "even the youngest students' responses exhibited a discriminating eye for features such as skin, hair, and eye color" (p. 402). Park's study has implications for early childhood educators, challenging them to examine how race, ethnic awareness, and cultural identity operate in their own lives, the lives of their young learners, and within the broader contexts where they teach.

Early childhood classrooms are designed to be developmentally appropriate and create a nurturing space for young children. Teachers at this level care for the whole child and teach a wide range of both academic and social skills. According to Strohmeier and Spiel (2012), "Cultural/ethnic identity is also a significant contributor to well-being, as individuals gain positive self-attitudes from belonging to groups that are meaningful to them" (p. 62). Nurturing the whole child includes recognizing differences and affirming diversity in the early childhood classroom. Teachers must meet the basic needs of the young children in their care by helping them develop a positive self-concept.

Self-concept is tied to racial and cultural awareness and pride. It is in the best interest of young children to have open and forthright conversations about racial and cultural markers. If these conversations are based on the portrayals of characters in books, teachers can carefully select images and stories that challenge stereotypes, lessen invisibility, and increase cultural competence. According to Kemple et al. (2016), in today's early childhood classrooms, the issue of race must be addressed through the "planned curriculum, spontaneous conversations, and cooperative activities which are designed with consideration of children's developmental level and their life experiences" (p. 99). From having diverse books available in the classroom to designing quality lessons around a specific title based on teachable moments, diverse children's literature is an ideal way to foster this kind of work.

Howard (2018) reminds early childhood educators that culture matters in instruction and classroom interactions for all learners, asserting that "the importance of culture in the learning process cannot be overstated" (p. 26). He goes on to argue for an early childhood curriculum that values each child and affords them the opportunity to bring their experiences to the classroom to make connections and build on their cultural capital or knowledge base. By utilizing the kinds of books highlighted in this chapter, teachers will be able to embrace Howard's recommendations. The books have been selected because they are forthright in describing differences, are likely to open doors to conversation, and focus on a child's perspective. Teachers who utilize these texts will find them to be authentic, accessible, and informative. These collections of books have the potential to foster greater understanding and enable students and teachers to see each other more clearly and fully.

## SHARING AND DISCUSSING DIFFERENCES

As the research above demonstrates, children who do not see themselves in the curricular materials or children's literature in their classrooms have compromised social and learning opportunities. As Purnell et al. (2007) explain, "Children feel emotionally secure when they find themselves, and those they love, positively represented in curriculum materials" (p. 424). The consequences of a lack of mirrors for children of color should not be underestimated. While Clark and Clark's (1947) landmark study of children's race-based doll preferences took place over seventy years ago, recent studies continue to show both African-American and white children favoring white dolls (Kemple et al., 2016; Liu et al., 2018). Alarcon et al. (2000) recently developed a new instrument to measure children's skin color preferences. Based on their use of the instrument with Puerto Rican children, preference for lighter skin color is not always tied to self-esteem. However, since it is confirmed that children are aware of skin color differences, it is likely that that low self-esteem is racialized, "such that children who feel less well about themselves associate it with skin color" (Alarcon et al., 2000, p. 219).

Children will notice racial and cultural differences around them; the question is how do they assign meaning to those differences, and how can teachers and curricular materials influence that process? When children encounter books that address these kinds of differences in the classroom, instruction can be designed to facilitate conversations that are natural and value the voices and perspectives of the readers. Young children are active participants in meaning construction in interactions with texts. Books that provide much-needed mirrors for children from diverse backgrounds need to be prioritized and valued by teachers as part of their approach to educating the whole child.

The Caldecott-winning *The Snowy Day* (Keats, 1962), which endures as a classic in children's literature, features a child of color without any mention of race or racial differences, but at the time of its release, it offered children long-overdue mirrors. *The Snowy Day* does not explore racial facets in its content, yet it still invited young children to reflect on race. In a 2012 NPR interview (Raz), Deborah Pope, the executive director of the Ezra Jack Keats Foundation, conveyed the following story:

> There was a teacher [who] wrote in to Ezra, saying, "The kids in my class, for the first time, are using brown crayons to draw themselves," Pope says. "These are African American children. Before this, they drew themselves with pink crayons. But now, they can see themselves."

Clearly, children are eager to see themselves in the books that surround them. There is power in just the mere images, but there is even more potential when books directly affirm children's physical traits and racial backgrounds. These are the books endorsed in this chapter and recommended for use by early childhood teachers as they nurture the whole child while validating racial, ethnic, and cultural identities. "Teachers and school play a critical role in helping children maintain a positive cultural identity while solidifying their sense of self as learners" (Fleming et al., 2016, p. 20). Using literature as a springboard for meaningful conversations is a pedagogically sound way to affirm students' sense of racial identity and self-awareness.

The metaphorical mirrors offered in these books enable teachers to provide young learners with neglected opportunities to see themselves in texts (Bishop, 1990, 2012; Botelho & Rudman, 2009). Research has shown that using these kinds of books promotes cultural understanding and critical thinking (Yenika-Agbaw & Napoli, 2011; Copenhaver-Johnson et al., 2007; DeNicolo & Franquiz, 2006). Exposure to books that provide mirrors as well as cultural authenticity and specificity empowers both students and teachers.

As Bishop (1982) explains, when authors and illustrators use language and colors that describe a range of skin tones, they are ascribing to an awareness of the "naturalness of such descriptions among Afro-Americans and perhaps indicative of an effort to create and promote positive associations with the darkness that carries so many negative connotations in the English language" (p. 71). Rather than avoiding discussion of the shades of skins and types of hair, teachers can fill their classrooms with books that celebrate those differences and bring the conversation into the classroom deliberately and supportively. The next section features a classroom vignette showcasing one teacher's integration of diverse literature to co-construct new understanding with her students.

Kindergarten teacher Miss K. recognized the need to incorporate culturally relevant and diverse literature within her early literacy curriculum. She noticed the limitations in her suburban school district's commercial reading program and sought to infuse literature that would affirm her students' cultural identities and promote conversations about race and gender while also meeting curricular needs. While Miss K. read various books with her class over a period of several months, this vignette highlights her students' responses to Monica Brown's (2011) *Marisol McDonald Doesn't Match*.

## CLASSROOM VIGNETTE:
## *MARISOL MCDONALD DOESN'T MATCH*

On a crisp fall morning, the kindergarten students in Miss K.'s class eagerly awaited the shared reading of *Marisol McDonald Doesn't Match* by Monica Brown. In this book, a young girl describes feeling both conflicted and proud of her seemingly contrasting identities. She has red hair and brown skin; she likes soccer and princesses; she's Peruvian and Scottish. Before reading the text, the class talked about the character and the title, then predicted what might take place. Miss K. recorded their predictions on the whiteboard and invited her students to listen for clues about why the title says that Marisol "doesn't match." Will Miss K.'s students notice the ways in which Marisol "doesn't match"?

Marisol's dilemmas throughout the story show her awareness of her racial and cultural differences. She is proud of these traits but also learns how to negotiate them in social contexts. *Marisol McDonald Doesn't Match* offers readers a character who is self-aware and growing in confidence. Sharing this book with young children opens the door to conversations about race, identity, individuality, and personal pride.

During the shared reading, students made observations about Marisol's individuality and strength of character. When Miss K. posed the question "How does Marisol feel about being "mismatched" at the beginning of the story?" her students (all names are pseudonyms) discussed their thoughts about Marisol's characteristics and feelings.

Kayla: Marisol is unique! I love her and think that she is just great.

Caleb: Yeah, me too. I think that she learns to love who she is.

Maddie: Some of her friends tease her because her clothes do not match, but she finds out it's okay to be who she is.

Joshua: Miss K., Marsol is my new favorite character.

Miss K.: I am glad to hear that you like Marisol McDonald. Tell me more about how her feelings changed.

Celia: Marisol is happy.

Miss K.: Thank you for sharing, Celia. Can you tell me more about why she is happy?

Celia: Yes, she is happy because she loves who she is no matter what.

Miss K.: Great job. What else can we learn from Marisol McDonald?

Joshua: To help us to be happy.

Kayla: To be yourself. This story made me feel good inside.

Celia: I learned that it's okay to do what you want even if it is different from other people.

The class then discussed the theme of staying true to yourself. Matthew added, "Miss K., you shared this story because you don't want us all to be the same." While Miss K. returned to the story several times during the week, her students grasped that the character of Marisol McDonald demonstrated pride in all aspects of her identity. Moving beyond her traditional literacy centers, Miss K. decided to incorporate technology in response to the story.

Using Audioboom, Miss K. recorded the story for her students to listen to a second time. Students then contributed their thoughts about the story on a graffiti board. The graffiti board was used for students to interpret the theme of the story through illustrations, speech bubbles, words, sentences, and symbols. According to Short et al. (1996), a graffiti board captures and explores "what's on students' minds" as they create meaning when responding to the text. During the post-discussion of the story, Miss K. led her class to discuss their responses to their collective graffiti board, as shown in figure 1.1. Some students enthusiastically shared their contributions. For example, John said, "I added a rainbow." Miss K. responded by asking, "Why did you choose a rainbow?" John replied, "Rainbows are colorful, and it is okay to be colorful. Just like Marisol McDonald."

In this example, the book *Marisol McDonald Doesn't Match* encouraged students to think critically about a diverse character. The next section includes multimodal text sets with annotations of books that can provide similar entry points for teachers to incorporate diverse books and support critical thinking in their curriculum. It is important to keep in mind that the collection of books and digital resources addresses different perspectives on the topic. Moreover, we provide suggestions that support culturally relevant literacy instruction. According to Ladson-Billings (1994), culturally relevant teaching is "pedagogy that empowers students intellectually, socially, emotionally, and politically by using cultural referents to impart knowledge, skills, and attitudes" (pp. 17–18). As early childhood educators begin to

**Figure 1.1.   Graffiti Wall Response to *Marisol McDonald Doesn't Match***

curate their collections, they should be sure to maintain high standards for quality for both diversity and literary merit to ensure balanced representation.

All books in this chapter were selected based on copyright date, literary quality, the role of illustrations, and the developmental appropriateness for the audience. Early children's books that present this kind of affirmation include *Black White Just Right* (Davol, 1993), *Black Is Brown Is Tan* (Adoff, 1973), and *Whitewash* (Shange, 1997). A bibliography at the end of the chapter includes these and additional related books that fit the theme. The text sets only include books that are likely to be available in school and public libraries and exclude books that are overwhelmingly didactic in tone. In addition, books featuring anthropomorphism or other metaphorical approaches to diversity were not included in this section since this chapter was focused on books that directly deal with physical differences and allow children to see themselves. The first text set includes books and activities that focus on self-love and affirmation, while the second set addresses conflicts that may arise in this context.

## MULTIMODAL TEXT SETS

### Text Set 1: Self-Awareness and Self-Love (Physical Traits, Hair, and Skin)

This text set highlights books for young readers that directly describe and celebrate physical traits such as variations in skin color. Books in this set feature photography or realistic illustrations rather than cartoon-style art. These books are joyful in tone and many have the potential to disrupt biased standards of beauty. The books pay homage to a wide range of physical traits and encourage both self-awareness and self-love.

Thomas, J. C. (2008). *Blacker the Berry*. Ill. by F. Cooper. New York, NY: Amistad.

This collection of poetry encourages children to see the beauty in all skin tones. Each poem features a child of color describing him- or herself in terms of skin color. One says, "I am midnight and berries" while another states "I am as light as snowberries in fall." A wordless page at the end shows all the children from the previous poems smiling and laughing together. The poems feature metaphors invoking the colors of the natural world and emphasize self-love in both the art and the text.

Johnson, D. (2007). *Hair Dance!* Ill. by K. Johnson. New York, NY: Henry Holt.

Similar to *Shades of People,* this book features photography on brightly colored backgrounds. The images and text focus on different hairstyles and textures. Children in the book love their hair, which is shown in a variety of styles, from braids to dreadlocks. Terms such as *Afro puffs* and *love locs* will be familiar to some readers and offer new cultural knowledge for others. This upbeat book embraces the idea of hair as works of art and points of pride.

Manushkin, F. (2015). *Happy in Our Skin*. Ill. by L. Tobia. Somerville, MA: Candlewick Press.

This rhyming picture book presents an array of diverse families in the illustrations while the text playfully describes the beauty of all types of skin. A range of skin colors are described (e.g., honey gold, cocoa brown), but other aspects of skin are addressed as well. One verse states, "Sometimes skin has freckles or birthmarks or dimples." The book invites readers to observe and reflect on their own skin and take pride in their physical traits.

Rotner, S. (2009). *Shades of People*. New York, NY: Holiday House.

This book functions as a photographic essay exploring and affirming the various shades of skin color in the children featured. Each page is covered in photographs with brief text describing skin tone and pointing out just how many shades exist. One line reminds children that "even in the same family there can be many shades." The last page features a photograph of sandy hands of children in shades from light to dark. Like the other books in this set, *Shades of People* offers points of comparison and acceptance for young children.

**Text Set 1: Multimodal Resources and Extension Activities**

The books in this set provide an opportunity for both playful and serious reflection on racial and cultural differences. Several of the books feature photography, which serves as an ideal springboard for teachers to invite children to make their own "photo-biographies" using an online scrapbooking tool such as Smilebox (www.smilebox.com) or the Pictello app. Teachers could also invite students to create digital stories about their unique qualities using platforms such as Little Bird Tales, Storybird, or the My Story School ebook-maker app.

Students can make comparisons and connections as they see the variations across the pictures. Comparisons and descriptions are a key to the literary style in these books about identity. Many of the books compare skin color to food or elements of nature. Use the text from a poetry collection such as *Blacker the Berry* (Thomas, 2008) for children to describe themselves and then digitally display their descriptors using a word cloud tool (https://wordart.com or https://worditout.com). These activities are appropriate for young children and build on literacy skills in the areas of vocabulary and writing. Some of the language in these texts may be unfamiliar to children so the class can investigate what a "huckleberry bush" looks like or look at (and taste) different types of honey. *Happy in Our Skin* (Manushkin, 2015) uses terms such as *birthmark* and *dimple*. Teachers can make interdisciplinary connections to science or health using videos such as http://kidshealth.org/en/kids/skin-movie.html.

A more playful approach to exploring and extending these books could include the use of videos and apps. Children could tell stories about their first haircuts and then use Toca Boca Hair Salon (https://tocaboca.com/app/toca-hair-salon) to imagine haircuts in a fantasy context, engaging the imagination and possibly inviting further reflection on differences. As teachers work to balance ways to help children see themselves and embrace their unique qualities, they may also find web resources such as Teaching Tolerance's "painting beauty" strategy helpful. In this strategy, teachers share self-portraits by famous artists to talk about how the subject saw themselves. Students make observations about the self-portraits and then create their own using a variety of materials (with mixing encouraged) to create their own self-portraits (www.tolerance.org/classroom-resources/tolerance-lessons/painting-beauty-creating-selfportraits).

## Text Set 2: Self-Confidence in Context: Respect for Self and Others

The books in this set also address racial and cultural differences; however, the focus is not simply on celebration and affirmation. In the books in this set, characters face challenges based on those differences and have to negotiate difficult contexts. Society sends mixed messages about what it means to be unique or different. Children may be proud of their backgrounds one day but then experience conflict the next. The stories in these books show children negotiating the complicated ways identities can create challenges and conflicts.

Wong, J. (2002). *Apple Pie Fourth of July*. Ill. by M. Chodos-Irvine. San Diego, CA: Harcourt.

The young protagonist in this book listens to the parade outside and tries to convince her parents that "Americans do not eat Chinese food on the Fourth of July." As a Chinese American, she is convinced that the holiday is one that will not involve their store. The conflict in the story seems to stem from the character's focus on what it means to be American and questions she has about being both Chinese and American. Customers do not come during the day for Chinese food, and in one scene, the little girl is using chopsticks to eat the food they made that no one came to order. But customers do come in the evening, and at the end of the book, the girl is shown using a fork to eat a slice of apple pie. *Apple Pie Fourth of July* focuses on the perspective of a child who is trying to understand her place in the community and her identity in a larger context.

Latham, I., & Waters, C. (2018). *Can I Touch Your Hair?* Ill. by S. Qualls & S. Alko. Minneapolis, MN: Carolrhoda Books.

This poetry collection explores the intersection between race, acceptance, and childhood friendships. The poems are based on each of the authors' personal childhood experiences and explore topics such as hair, school, church, and hobbies. Each poem provides a starting point for deeper conversations with students, colleagues, families, and friends. Alko and Qualls's mixed media illustrations support and reflect the emotional quality of each poem. This collection provides a different perspective, opening a door to reflect on privilege and unrecognized bias.

Cherry, M. (2019). *Hair Love*. Ill. by V. Harrison. New York, NY: Kokila.

Zuri wakes up and decides to give her dad a break by doing her hair herself for a special day. When she wears braids, she feels like a princess, and when she wears her hair in two puffs, she feels like a superhero, but what will she do today? The pictures show Zuri looking online for ideas, but then her dad comes to help her. They try several styles and finally decide on "funky puff buns!" Zuri's dad perfects the style and then she dons a cape to greet her mother, who is returning from a trip at the door. Zuri's mom hair is in a wrap and her dad has dreadlocks. The final page shows the family of three (and the cat, Rocky) taking a selfie and proudly embracing hair love.

Brown, M. (2011). *Marisol McDonald Doesn't Match*. Ill. by S. Palacios. San Francisco, CA: Children's Books Press.

Marisol McDonald celebrates her multiracial background and displays her individuality by wearing mismatched clothes and staying true to her creative spirit. She is consistently teased by her family and peers and decides to conform to the norm. Marisol's art teacher presents her with a note with a much-needed positive message that boosts her self-esteem: "The Marisol McDonald that I know is a creative, unique, bilingual, Peruvian-Scottish-American, soccer-playing artist and simply marvelous!" In this spirited bilingual story, Marisol navigates how to accept her individuality.

**Text Set 2: Multimodal Activities and Extensions**

The books in this set explore characters who navigate storyworlds where their identities are questioned. Through various circumstances, the characters strengthen their sense of self and understand their identity better. In order to facilitate a culturally responsive classroom that nurtures, supports, and enhances the learning of all students, it is critical that teachers engage in self-reflection and dialogue to understand their personal attitudes, uncover their biases, and develop cultural sensitivity by learning about the variety of students and families within the early childhood program. Teachers can foster safe environments for students to understand, regulate, and express their emotions by using social dramatic play to support children's emotional development while also providing a space for them to express and cope with feelings. Using selected poems from *Can I Touch Your Hair: Poems of Race, Mistakes, and Friendship* (Latham & Waters, 2018), students can dramatize the poems, discuss their feelings and personal experiences, and then write individual poems. Students could also use various media to illustrate their poems, or they can create digital collage using images from Creative Commons (https://creativecommons.org) or their individual artwork.

The picture books also present opportunities for teachers to explore character traits while enhancing their comprehension skills. Students can create character-poems, character vokis (www.voki.com), or Venn diagrams to compare and contrast the characters. Students can also learn about the author's writing style and purpose for creating their work by working in groups to conduct an author study. Opportunities to study an author's work will prompt further conversations about how the author's cultural background and identity carry throughout their body of work. Teachers can incorporate video clips within their literacy centers or before read-aloud selections.

- Monica Brown reads aloud *Marisol McDonald Doesn't Match:* www.youtube.com/watch?v=uvPJCswViel
- Janet Wong discusses the premise behind *Apple Pie Fourth of July*: www.youtube.com/watch?v=SlBuvwVHN44
- Animated short of *Hair Love*: www.youtube.com/watch?v=kNw8V_Fkw28

## Additional Recommended Books about Self

> Adoff, A. (1982). *All the Colors of the Race*. Ill. by J. Steptoe. New York, NY: Lothrop, Lee & Shepard.
> al Serkal, M., & Luciani, R. (2019). *Mira's Curly Hair*. London, UK: Lantana Publishing Ltd.
> Alko, S. (2009). *I'm Your Peanut Butter Big Brother*. New York, NY: Knopf.
> Barnes, D. (2017). *Crown: Ode to the Fresh Cut*. Ill. by G. C. James. Chicago, IL: Bolden.

Britt, P. (2017). *Why Am I Me?* Ill. by S. Qualls & S. Alko. New York, NY: Scholastic.
Cisneros, S. (1994). *Hairs/Pelitos*. Ill. by T. Ybanez. New York, NY: Random House.
Cole, H. (2005). *Am I a Color Too?* Ill. by G. Purnell. Bellevue, WA: Illumination Arts.
Diggs, T. (2011). *Chocolate Me*. Ill. by S. Evans. New York, NY: Feiwel and Friends.
Diggs. T. (2015). *Mixed Me*. Ill. by S. Evans. New York, NY: Feiwel and Friends.
Evans, K. (2011). *What's Special about Me, Mama?* Ill. by J. Steptoe. New York, NY: Hyperion.
Fields, M. (2019). *Honeysmoke*. Ill. by Y. Moises. New York, NY: Imprint.
Franklin, A. (2019). *Not Quite Snow White*. Ill. by E. Glenn. New York, NY: HarperCollins.
Freeman, M. (2019). *Hair, It's a Family Affair*. London, UK: Cassava Republic.
Grimard, G. (2016). *Lila and the Crow*. Toronto, Canada: Annick Press.
Hong, J. (2017). *Lovely*. Berkeley, CA: Creston Books.
hooks, b. (2004). *Skin Again*. Ill. by C. Raschka. New York, NY: Hyperion.
Iyengar, M. M. (2009). *Tan to Tamarind*. San Francisco, CA: Children's Book Press.
Katz, K. (1999). *The Colors of Us*. New York, NY: Henry Holt and Company.
Lester, J. (2005). *Let's Talk about Race*. Ill. by K. Barbour. New York, NY: HarperCollins.
Miller, S. (2018). *Don't Touch My Hair!* New York, NY: Little, Brown and Company.
Muhamma, I., & Ali, S. K. (2019). *The Proudest Blue*. Ill. by H. Aly. New York, NY: Little, Brown & Company.
Nyong'o, L. (2019). *Sulwe*. Ill. by V. Harrison. New York, NY: Simon & Schuster.
Pinkney, S. (2006). *Shades of Black*. Ill. by M. Pinkney. New York, NY: Scholastic.
Richards., D. (2017). *What's the Difference?: Being Different Is Amazing*. New York, NY: Feiwel & Friends.
Roe, R. M. (2019). *Happy Hair*. New York, NY: Doubleday Books.
Tarpley, N. (2017, 1998). *I Love My Hair!* Ill. by E. B. Lewis. New York, NY: Little, Brown & Company.
Thompkins-Bigelow, J. (2018). *Mommy's Khimar*. Ill. by E. Glenn. New York, NY: Simon & Schuster.

Tyler, M. (2005). *The Skin You Live In*. Ill. by D. Csicsko. Chicago, IL: Chicago Children's Museum.

Winters, K. (2016). *French Toast*. Ill. by F. Thisdale. Toronto, Canada: Pajama Press.

## AUTHOR SPOTLIGHT: INTERVIEW WITH JANET WONG

Janet Wong—poet, author, speaker, and publisher—has published more than thirty books for young people, including picture books, novels, poetry, and professional resources. She is the recipient of many distinctions, including the International Literacy Association's Celebrate Literacy Award and the Lee Bennett Hopkins Award Honor for Poetry. Wong's long-standing commitment to the profession includes service to the National Council of Teachers of English (NCTE) Commission on Literature, the NCTE Excellence in Children's Poetry Award Committee, the NCTE Children's Literature Assembly Board, and the International Literacy Association's Notable Books for a Global Society Committee. Along with her colleague, Dr. Sylvia Vardell, they have created the Poetry Friday Anthology Series aligned to the Common Core Standards. More information about the series and Janet Wong can be found at http://pomelobooks.com and www.janetwong.com.

*1. Please share your thinking about the importance of multicultural literature in the early childhood classroom.*

I think it's particularly important to share a wide variety of *words* from other languages, not just the larger idea of "cultures." Young children need to hear Spanish, Chinese, Arabic, Tagalog, Somali, Russian, Italian, and Irish Gaelic—the more, the better! The way to become a truly inclusive world is for everyone to feel that they belong in—and belong to—many places. This is why I love a poem like "How to Make a Friend" by Jane Heitman Healy (from *The Poetry Friday Anthology for Celebrations*), a poem that asks young readers to reach out and say hello to a new friend in half a dozen languages.

*2. Some multicultural books affirm and explore identity. Explain how you do this in your books.*

In *Apple Pie Fourth of July*, probably my best-known book, a Chinese American girl is ashamed of her immigrant parents, mini-mart owners who cook Chinese food even on the Fourth of July. And so, she is shocked—but delighted—when, in the early evening, customers start coming into the store to buy chow mein and sweet-and-sour pork. I wrote this book based on something that actually happened in my family. My parents owned Tri City Market in rural Oregon. I was already an adult, living in Seattle at the time; I called my parents to wish them a happy fourth. When my father told me that he'd cooked Chinese food to sell on the 4th, I said, "Hello? This is the Fourth of July—an all-American holiday—and you're cooking Chinese food?" The people of Myrtle Creek surprised me by choosing Chinese dinners for Independence Day; I wrote this book as a way of admitting that I was thinking too narrowly. I've been told that this book has inspired many lively classroom discussions—and leads to a sharp increase in the number of non-Asian kids seeking out Chinese food on the fourth!

*3. Select one of your favorite books or poems, and share how you would explore it with young learners.*

A favorite book that I've been involved with is *The Poetry Friday Anthology for Celebrations,* an anthology created by my colleague Sylvia Vardell and I that features the work of 115 poets, and 156 poems about everything from the Dashain festival of Nepal to Diwali (Deepavali) to Día de los Muertos to the International Day of Persons with Disabilities. I'm really proud of the way we present so much happy diversity—the way we make kids want to know more about different cultural celebrations. How would I explore it with young learners? I would follow the five steps outlined for each poem in the teacher/librarian edition. Sylvia Vardell's "Take 5!" mini-lessons make it easy to share poetry!

*4. What advice would you give early childhood teachers as they attempt to explore concepts of identity with young children through multicultural literature?*

When Alma Flor Ada and F. Isabel Campoy met with me and Sylvia Vardell to suggest that we make *The Poetry Friday Anthology for Celebrations* a fully bilingual Spanish-English book (which we ultimately did; all 156 poems are presented both in Spanish and English), I said, "Yes, that would be really terrific for the Spanish-speaking kids." Alma Flor Ada corrected me in a way I'll never forget. She said, "It will be terrific for *all* of the kids." So my advice would be: Don't hesitate to read a poem in Spanish to the whole class, even if no one speaks Spanish. You will be helping to form identities of inclusion for these children. And if you don't speak Spanish, invite a guest reader, or play the free SoundCloud bilingual readings of these poems from your computer (find a link at PomeloBooks.com). A particularly great choice to play aloud is the poem "Bilingual"/"Bilingüe" by Alma Flor Ada, which you can hear here: https://soundcloud.com/user-862117714/bilingual?in=user-862117714/sets/bilingual-performances.

*5. What classroom suggestions can you provide for teachers to select and incorporate diverse books into their curriculum?*

Poetry is great for fitting into your busy schedule: it takes just a minute to share a poem. Sharing five to six selections from a diverse anthology is an easy way to take a five-minute tour of the world! You don't have to limit yourself to picture books and novels—and you certainly don't have to incorporate a whole book at a time. Read a few pages of a handful of nonfiction books—tidbits to whet the appetites of your students—and then hand out slips of paper with the titles of the books and cover images, so their families can find those books at the library.

*6. What are your hopes and dreams for early childhood classrooms and libraries in the future?*

I would love to see whole classes from different parts of the country (and world) Skyping together on a regular basis to share poems. Just five minutes of children from different demographics waving and sharing with each other once a week, hearing each other's voices.

*7. Some teachers are hesitant to talk about diversity with young children. What words of encouragement can you offer them?*

Kids usually love what's most familiar to them. Some of the diverse and inclusive selections that you share might not be their favorites at first; if that's the case, no problem. They don't have to adore every book or poem you read. If your kids wanted to eat only cotton candy and potato chips all week, would you let them do that? Hopefully not! You'd want to see some balance in their diets. Let's see that our kids also have balanced reading diets, too!

# REFERENCES

Aboud, F. E. (1988). *Children and prejudice.* New York, NY: Blackwell.
Aboud, F. E. (2003). The formation of in-group favoritism and outgroup prejudice in young children: Are they distinct attitudes? *Developmental Psychology, 39*(1), 48–60.
Alarcon, O., Szalacha, L. A., Erkut, S., Fields, J. P., & Coil, C. G. (2000). The color of my skin: A measure to assess children's perceptions of their skin color. *Applied Developmental Science, 4*(4), 208–221.
Bishop, R. S. (1982). *Shadow and substance: Afro-American experience in contemporary children's fiction.* Urbana, IL: National Council of Teachers of English.
Bishop, R. S. (1990). Mirrors, windows and sliding glass doors. *Perspectives, 6*(3), ix–xi.
Bishop, R. S. (2012). Reflections on the development of African American children's literature. *Journal of Children's Literature, 38*(2), 5–13.
Botelho, M. J., & Rudman, M. K. (2009). *Critical multicultural analysis of children's literature: Mirrors, windows, and doors.* New York, NY: Routledge.
Boutte, G. S., Lopez-Robertson, J., & Powers-Costello, E. (2011). Moving beyond colorblindness in early childhood classrooms. *Early Childhood Education Journal, 39*(5), 335–342.
Clark, K. B., & Clark, M. K. (1947). Racial identification and preference in Negro children. In T. M. Newcomb & E. L. Hartley (Eds.), *Readings in social psychology* (pp. 169–178). London, UK: Methuen.

Copenhaver-Johnson, J. F., Bowman, J. T., & Johnson, A. C. (2007). Santa stories: Children's inquiry about race during picturebook read-alouds. *Language Arts, 84*(4), 234–244.

Delpit, L. (2012). *"Multiplication is for white people": Raising expectations for other people's children.* New York, NY: The New Press.

DeNicolo, C. P., & Franquiz, M. E. (2006). "Do I have to say it?": Critical encounters with multicultural children's literature. *Language Arts, 84*(2), 157–170.

Derman-Sparks, L., LeeKeenan, D., & Nimmo, J. (2015). *Leading anti-bias early childhood programs: A guide for change.* New York, NY: Teachers College Press; Washington, DC: National Association for the Education of Young Children (NAEYC).

Derman-Sparks, L., & Ramsey, P. (2011). *What if all the kids are white? Anti-bias multicultural education with young children and families* (2nd ed.). New York, NY: Teachers College Press.

Earick, M. E. (2009). *Racially equitable teaching: Beyond the whiteness of professional development for early childhood educators.* New York, NY: Peter Lang.

Fleming, J., Catapano, S., Thompson, C., & Carillo, S. R. (2016). *More mirrors in the classroom: Using urban children's literature to increase literacy.* Lanham, MD: Rowman & Littlefield Publishers.

Howard, T. C. (2018). Capitalizing on culture: Engaging young learners in diverse classrooms. *YC Young Children, 73*(2), 24–33.

Kemple, K., Lee, I., & Harris, M. (2016). Young children's curiosity about physical differences associated with race: Shared reading to encourage conversation. *Early Childhood Education Journal, 44*(2), 97–105.

Ladson-Billings, G. (1994). The dreamkeepers: Successful teaching for African-American students. San Francisco: Jossey-Bass.

Liu, S., Quinn, P. C., Xiao, N. G., Wu, Z., Liu, G., & Lee, K. (2018). Relations between scanning and recognition of own- and other-race faces in 6- and 9-month-old infants. *PsyCh Journal, 7*(2), 92–102.

Marion, M. (2011). *Guidance of young children* (8th ed.). Upper Saddle River, NJ: Pearson Education.

Park, C. C. (2011). Children making sense of racial and ethnic differences: A sociocultural approach. *American Educational Research Journal, 48*(2), 387–420.

Purnell, P., Ali, P., Begum, N., & Carter, M. (2007). Windows, bridges and mirrors: Building culturally responsive early childhood classrooms through the integration of literacy and the arts. *Early Childhood Education Journal, 34*(6), 419–424.

Ramsey, P. G. (2009). Growing up with contradictions of race and class. In E. L. Essa & M. M. Burnham (Eds.), *Informing our practice: Useful research on young children's development* (pp. 13–21). Washington, DC: National Association for the Education of Young Children.

Raz, G. (Host). (2012, January 28). The Snowy day: Breaking color barriers [Radio broadcast episode]. Retrieved from www.npr.org/2012/01/28/145052896/the-snowy-day-breaking-color-barriers-quietly

Short, K. G., Harste, J. C., & Burke, C. L. (1996). *Creating classrooms for authors and inquirers.* Portsmouth, NH: Heinemann.

Strohmeier, D., & Spiel, C. (2012). Peer relations amongst immigrant adolescents: Some methodological problems and key findings. In M. Messer, R. Schroeder, & R. Wodak (Eds.), *Migrations: Interdisciplinary perspectives* (pp. 57–65). New York, NY: Springer.

Tatum, B. D. (2003). *"Why are all the Black kids sitting together in the cafeteria?" and other conversations about race.* New York, NY: Basic Books.

Winkler, E. N. (2009). Children are not colorblind: How young children learn race. *PACE: Practical Approaches for Continuing Education, 3*(3), 1–8.

Yenika-Agbaw, V., & Napoli, M. (Eds.). (2011). *African and African American children's and adolescent literature in the classroom: A critical guide.* New York, NY: Peter Lang.

## Additional Children's Literature Cited

Adoff, A. (1973/2002). *Black is brown is tan.* Ill. by E. A. McCully. New York, NY: Harper Collins.

Brown, M. (2011). *Marisol McDonald doesn't match*. Ill. by S. Palacios. San Francisco, CA: Children's Books Press.
Davol, M. (1993). *Black white, just right.* Ill by I. Trivas. Morton Grove, IL: Albert Whitman.
Keats, E. (1962). *The snowy day*. New York, NY: Viking Press.
Shange, N. (1997). *Whitewash.* Ill. by N. Sporn. New York, NY: Walker and Company.

*Chapter Two*

# Partnering at Home

*Knowing Your Family*

- How do the families portrayed in children's books correlate with the realities of families in our classrooms today?
- In what ways can diverse children's books promote dialogue about various family structures?
- To what extent can teachers enhance family-to-school partnerships using high-quality literature featuring diverse families?

According to the National Association for the Education of Young Children (NAEYC), early childhood education programs should forge collaborative relationships with the families of the children in their programs. These relationships should be "sensitive to family composition" and teachers and staff should "talk with families about their family structure" (NAEYC, 2005). Teachers and caregivers know that parents and families are integral to the well-being and development of young children. Preschool teachers have contact with parents/guardians on a daily basis while early elementary teachers strive to involve parents in activities and ongoing learning projects. Best practices focus on inviting and encouraging children to share about their experiences outside of school, and the classroom community needs to be prepared for a range of family structures.

While the majority (69 percent) of America's 73.7 million children under age eighteen live in families with two parents, teachers will also encounter children living in different kinds of households (U.S. Census Bureau, 2016). These might include single-parent families, LGBTQ families, widowed or divorced parents, and blended families. In addition, even "conventional" two-parent families might include adoptive or foster families and interracial families. Teachers may take for granted that they are inclusive of the family types in their classrooms, but subtle forms of bias are often in play. For instance, do the forms sent home include "mother's name" and "father's name" rather than "parent/guardian name"? Does the school focus on gender-exclusive events such as "donuts with dads?" Are children asked to draw their house instead of "where they sleep?" Are students likely to see families like theirs in books, images, or other media they are exposed to in school? This chapter focuses on books that teachers can use to create an inclusive classroom culture by diversifying their book selections and designing instruction that affirms children from a range of family types.

Professional standards for early childhood educators recognize that children need to have a chance to learn that families have a variety of structures and that "preschool and kindergarten children are ready to engage in discussions about fairness, friendship, responsibility, authority, and differences" (NAEYC, 2010, p. 30). Rather than minimizing family differences and possibly creating a deficit model about family types, teachers with the best interests of children in mind will find ways to include and normalize all family structures. Instead of turning to books that address family differences metaphorically or through fantasy devices, we recommend books that are straightforward in tone and accurate in description.

The picture books selected for this chapter are mostly realistic fiction, portraying families in contemporary and everyday contexts. A few of the books fall into the genre of nonfiction, but those still capture typical experiences of families. Books with fantasy elements or anthropomorphism were not included because we want to encourage teachers to directly address real family structures, rather than metaphorical ones. For instance, *Spork* (Maclear, 2010) features a "family" with a mother portrayed as a spoon and a father portrayed as a fork. Other popular titles such as *The Family Book* (Parr, 2003) and *Families Families Families* (Lang & Lang, 2015) offer playful and inclusive treatments of family differences but with more imaginative and unrealistic elements. The books included in this collection were selected to empower teachers to talk in an accurate and accepting way about family composition. Making variations in family types visible and valued will make it possible for all students to participate in activities such as telling stories from home, creating gifts for parents/guardians, inviting caregivers into the classroom, exploring family connections, completing writing activities, and bringing in "brag bags" or show-and-tell items.

## WHAT KINDS OF FAMILIES ARE PORTRAYED?

For the purposes of this chapter, a careful and exhaustive search of picture books was conducted to find the best books with family diversity. Unfortunately, quality picture books with children living in foster families or with extended family caregivers such as grandparents and other relatives were lacking. More than 2.5 million grandparents now raise grandchildren without a biological parent present in the home (Simmons & Dye, 2003) and according to the U.S. Census Bureau, 9 percent of all children live with at least one grandparent present (Kreider, 2011). In 2016, the Children's Bureau reported that over 400,000 children were in foster care (Child Welfare Information Gateway). This captures the essence of the mirrors and windows metaphor related to diverse books. Considering the current publishing trends, children being raised by grandparents or living with foster families will be denied books that serve as mirrors. In addition, multiracial children under the age of eighteen are the fastest-growing demographic in the country (Lee & Bean, 2012), yet the number of books featuring children with these backgrounds is still minimal. Children who live in families like these deserve rich and authentic books that reflect their experiences and are high quality and widely available.

Books featuring the following kinds of families were evaluated and selected based on quality, availability, and appropriateness: divorced or single parent families, LGBTQ families, interracial families, adoptive families, families experiencing trauma or loss (death of a parent and incarcerated parents). Books about other kinds of issues a family might face, such as homelessness, aging grandparents, or new siblings, will be presented in later chapters. Books that feature a range of families are also included in these sets. These collections are designed to show family diversity and explicitly name variations in family structures. These books are essential to the text sets in this chapter because of the lack of books featuring some of the family types. Many of the recommended titles involve more than one aspect of diversity, thus addressing the importance of intersectionality. The term *intersectionality* was developed by Crenshaw (1989) and earned this entry into the *Oxford English Dictionary* in 2015: "the interconnected nature of social categorizations such as race, class, and gender, regarded as creating overlapping and interdependent systems of discrimination or disadvantage" ("Intersectionality," n.d.). This concept is essential to understanding and using the books in this chapter. Some of these books include LGBTQ or adoptive families, but even the interracial books that feature "traditional" two-parent families are important to highlight because there is a great dearth of books portraying interracial families. A child with adoptive parents may struggle more with that difference than they do with having LGBTQ parents. A biological child of interracial LGBTQ parents may encounter more difficulty with homophobia than with racism.

In most cases the overlap in the kinds of challenges students from families like these might face will be impossible to separate out. Therefore, the need for books portraying a wide range of family types is so important, which is why a rich collection that includes books with varied styles or treatments should be sought out by those working with young children. Books with diverse family portrayals can be serious or silly. Family differences can be the focus of the book or less central to the plot and theme of the story. A good example of this is *Baby's First Words* (Engel, 2017), which is a concept book with tabs designed to teach familiar vocabulary but happens to feature an interracial two-dad family. This is an important book because the topic is not solely about family structure, but the inclusiveness makes the book unique and worthwhile. Similarly, while single-parent-family books were limited, the ones included here feature plotlines that are simple and universal.

Chaudhri (2017) found that picture books depicting multiracial characters, "although few in number, span the spectrum from being didactically overt in tackling mixed race experiences, to integrating that element with other issues to making no mention at all in the text, but leaving it to the reader to notice or not the visual depictions of people" (p. 23). This is true of many of the other sets of books in this chapter. The number of multiracial children is growing. According to a report by the Pew Research Center (Livingston, 2015) in 1970, only 1 percent of babies lived with two interracial parents. That number rose to 10 percent by 2013, and currently, 46 percent of all multiracial Americans are younger than eighteen. Studies have shown that biracial children are often invisible in classrooms and curricula (Baxley, 2008; Scanlon-McMath & King, 2011; Wardle & Cruz-Janzen, 2004). These children have the right to books that simply capture their joys and experiences and books that address struggles they may face. Teachers should strive for a balance in terms of how books take on or portray family diversity, with some offering broad representation and some that tell stories related to the differences.

It has been well-established that children need to see themselves in the books they encounter and that there is not an adequate number of diverse books available. While simply matching the percentage of diverse books to the population is not the goal, a concerted effort is needed to provide children with books that reflect their family situations—even if that situation is not a dominant one according to demographics. According to the U.S. Census Bureau (2018), the second most common (23 percent) family arrangement is children living with a single parent. In 2017, it was documented that one quarter (25 percent) of children under eighteen live with one parent. The percentage of children living with one parent who live with just their father saw an increase from 12.5 percent in 2007 to 16.1 percent in 2017. Yet teachers will find it difficult to find books that feature these family types in appealing picture books for young readers. Using these text sets is one way teachers can remedy that invisibility through positive and engaging portrayals of single parents.

Another group of families that might be marginalized or more directly discriminated against in school contexts are the "more than six million lesbian, gay, bisexual, transgender, and queer (LGBTQ) parents that are sending children to school" (Evans-Santiago & Lin, 2016, p. 56). There are an estimated 14 million children with LGBTQ families in the United States (Gates, 2013). These families may vary in how they are formed and how their households function. Children from LGBTQ families may be adopted or biological; they may have a single parent, two same-sex parents, or a stepfamily; they may come from interracial families or be biracial. The landmark picture book *Heather Has Two Mommies* (Newman) was published in 1989, opening the door to stories about LGBTQ families for young children. However, it was not until 2010—when the American Library Association's Stonewall Awards were expanded to include children's and young adult literature—that a major award was designated for this category of books. This demonstrated the long struggle to improve the quality and availability of books with LGBTQ themes; the struggle is more pronounced with regard to picture books. Perhaps the most widely known picture book is about penguins rather than humans. *And Tango Makes Three* (Richardson & Parnell, 2005) has frequently been challenged while also garnering many awards and commercial success. The collection presented in this chapter relies on only human portrayals in order to help connect with readers who have similar families. One reason for this is because children from LGBTQ families "sometimes experience mistreatment or lack of knowledge from practitioners or administrators" (Evans-Santiago & Lin, 2016, p. 57). The books selected excel at directly countering heteronormative perspectives and truly celebrate the joys of LGBTQ families.

Children from LGBTQ families and many of the other family types discussed in this chapter often find their experiences overlooked or diminished in classroom and social interactions. Parents, teachers, and peers make assumptions about families, and children often have to explain or correct others. A child of two dads might be asked about their mom while an adopted child might have to explain that their parents aren't "fake." Gajda's (2004) research found that families formed by adoption are often perceived as inferior. Yet one out of every twenty-five U.S. families with children have an adopted child ("Adoption Network," n.d.). Adoptive families are formed in a range of ways, including foster care, transnational adoption, and domestic open adoptions. Teachers may not find out right away that a child in their class was adopted, although "because adopted children are usually very wanted children, teachers are likely to find committed parents who will welcome the teacher as an ally" (Greenberg, 2001, p. 91). Children adopted internationally may want to learn more about their countries of origin, and some adopted children may want to celebrate their adoption day in school. These are opportunities for teachers to create an inclusive and open environment, but they also need to be prepared for adopted children who may experience harsh questions or bullying around their family structure (Greenberg, 2001; Smith-D'Arezzo, 2018; Gajda, 2004). Children whose families were formed through adoption deserve a range of books, some that simply portray and affirm their experience but also ones that capture some of the conflicts and complexities of adoption.

Children whose families experience difficulties due to death or incarceration will likely also have to face harsh questions from friends, teachers, and even the broader community. In the United States, one in twenty-five children has a parent incarcerated on any given day while approximately one in twelve children will have a parent incarcerated at some point during their life (Wildeman et al., 2018). Murphy and Cooper (2015) state that "five million children, representing seven percent of all U.S. children, have ever had a parent who lived with them go to jail or prison" (p. 1). Educators may not be aware that members of their students' families have been in prison. The immediate, direct, and overwhelming impact that this traumatic experience has on a child must be addressed. Teachers, caregivers, social workers, counselors, and local agencies have extended resources to provide support.

As schools and their students struggle with these challenges, trauma-informed care has emerged as a partial measure for intervention. Restoring and maintaining a vital relationship between incarcerated family members and their children is of paramount importance to the child's emotional well-being. As such, teachers can infuse selections of literature, such as the ones described in this chapter, to help readers know that they are not alone. Not all children and their caretakers are open about the incarceration of a parent (Nesmith & Ruhland, 2008). As a result, educators may not be aware that a student has a parent in prison. In other cases, an educator may be aware of the parent's incarceration, but the absence may not be discussed by the child or the caretaker. Educators need to be respectful of the caretaker's preferences regarding the issue; if the parent's incarceration becomes an issue at school, educators should communicate with the caretaker. Reading and responding to literature has been identified as a powerful method for dealing with traumatic events, such as losing a loved one (Dutro, 2008). Using children's literature to support a child who is experiencing grief can validate emotions and experiences (Copenhaver-Johnson et al., 2008; Corr, 2003–2004). Children whose families may not want to talk about this aspect of their lives still have to interact with peers in the classroom and navigate questions about their homes and parents.

Another aspect of family diversity that emerges from a traumatic event relates to children who have lost a parent. These children will also fall into the category of single-parent families, but they face unique differences and challenges. How should a classroom or school community respond when a parent dies? Children will have questions, and the child experiencing the loss will need help navigating their interactions with peers and adults. Anecdotal reports suggest that books can help children work through the experience of loss (Polak, 2007). Research on grief and loss demonstrates that children need time and guidance on how to deal with their feelings and that literature can be an important part of this process (Corr, 2010; Short, 2011). Any child going through a transition or change in their family could benefit from books that realistically and warmly portray aspects of the experience.

These text sets for family diversity attempt to be as inclusive and comprehensive as possible. However, the taken-for-granted images of "nuclear" or traditional families continue to dominate children's literature. Early childhood teachers will need to actively seek out books and informed critiques as they build a classroom collection. Some books are simple and straightforward, stating the facts about the various types of families in the world. Others are longer and may need to be mediated more deliberately due to the elements of sadness, loss, and confusion in some of the stories.

Table 2.1 shows the organization of the recommended books for this chapter by the family type featured. Many of the titles are diverse in more than one way. An LGBTQ book may also feature an adoptive family, while a divorced family may also be interracial. Books have been isolated into one category for the purposes of balance and based on the focus of the story. Not all of the books in this chart are included in the text sets; the best or most unique books were selected for the focused summaries and activities. In addition, each text set is balanced in terms of the types of families represented and the target audience. Additional recommended books are included at the end of the chapter.

One of the books that features a range of family types is *A Family Is a Family Is a Family* (O'Leary, 2016). While the book does not have a specific focus on adoption, the book was shared as part of a child's adoption day celebration in a second grade classroom. This classroom vignette captures how eager children are to share their family stories and the way books can serve as a way to facilitate curiosity, affirm differences, and build community.

## CLASSROOM VIGNETTE: *A FAMILY IS A FAMILY IS A FAMILY*

In a second grade classroom, a young boy has decided to celebrate his adoption day with his class by having his mom come for a classroom visit and share a read-aloud with the students. Andre and his classmates in Mrs. C's class will enjoy a snack together after the read-aloud. The book *A Family Is a Family Is a Family* (O'Leary, 2016) has been selected for the read-aloud so the classroom teacher can make a curricular connection to a family tree activity. It is April and the students in this class know each other well. In

Table 2.1. Recommended Books by Family Type

| Book | Family Types |
|---|---|
| Daddy, Papa, and Me<br>Donovan's Big Day<br>Baby's First Words<br>Harriet Gets Carried Away<br>Heather Has Two Mommies (new edition)<br>Mommy, Mama, and Me<br>Stella Brings the Family<br>A Tale of Two Daddies<br>A Tale of Two Mommies | LGBTQ |
| Made for Me<br>Saturday<br>Pecan Pie Baby<br>Kate and Nate Are Running Late<br>Possible: Ask Me, Invisible String, Side by Side | Single Parent |
| Fred Stays with Me<br>Emily's Blue Period<br>Monday, Wednesday, and Every Other Weekend<br>I Have Two Homes<br>Living with Mom and Dad<br>A Day with Dad | Divorce |
| Blackout<br>You Were the First<br>Hello Goodbye Window<br>I Love Saturdays y Domingos<br>I'm Your Peanut Butter Big Brother<br>Maisie's Scrapbook<br>One Word from Sophia<br>Airport Book | Interracial/Cross-Cultural |
| Our Gracie Aunt<br>Star of the Week<br>Ten Days and Nine Nights<br>A Most Unusual Day<br>I'm Adopted<br>My Mei Mei | Adoption/Foster Care |
| Knock Knock<br>Visiting Day<br>The Scar<br>My Father's Arms Are a Boat<br>Paula Knows What to Do<br>Far Apart, Close In Heart | Families in Transition/Trauma<br>Death and Incarceration |

| | Collections |
|---|---|
| *Family* (Monk) | |
| *Families* (Kuklin) | |
| *Families* (Rotner) | |
| *One Family* | |
| *Great Big Book of Families* (Hoffman) | |
| *A Family Is a Family Is a Family* | |
| *What a Family* | |
| *Monday Is One Day* | |
| *Who's in My Family* | |
| *My Friends and Me* | |

fact, they have been together as a class since kindergarten as part of a Spanish-immersion program, so the students already know a lot about each other's families. In the opening pages of *A Family Is a Family Is a Family*, a classroom teacher asks students what makes their families special. The illustrations show twelve children taking turns talking about their families with examples and confidence while one child waits hesitantly for her turn. As Andre's mom reads the book aloud, students are invited to offer comparisons to their own families.

On one page of the book, a child speaks of how her parents have been best friends since first grade, and states, "They really like each other. It's kind of gross." This makes the students in Andre's class laugh out loud. On another page, the child in the book explains, "Both my moms are terrible singers. And they both like to sing really loud." Students in the class laugh and share stories of how their parents are bad dancers, bad drivers, and bad cooks.

Another child in the book says, "We all look alike in my family. We just kind of go together." This prompts a whole class conversation about adoption.

Paul: I look like my mom but not my dad. My sister looks like my dad.

Sofia: Everyone says I'm the spitting image of my mom.

Emanny: Can you look like your mom even if you're adopted?

Mom: Some people say Andre and I look alike, but I don't think it really matters. What do you think?

Emanny: He kind of looks like you, but it's hard to say for sure.

As the book continues, there is a child that explains, "Some people say I look like my dad and some people say I look like my mom. I think I look like myself." The class conversation returns to the question of family resemblance.

Paul: If I cut my hair, I might look more like my dad. It's my curly hair that makes me look like my mom.

Elicia: Some people confuse me and my sister because we look so much alike.

Guadalupe: I'm dark like my mom, but my brother isn't.

The book moves on to a page with a child raised by a grandmother. She says that sometimes strangers think she's her mother instead of grandmother. The class starts to share similar stories.

Max: Everyone thinks my older sister is my mom!

Julian: My mom looks younger than my sister.

Andre: Once when we were out, someone thought my aunt was my mom's mom.

Mom: Yeah, Aunt Lauren is ten years older than me and she gets mistaken as Andre's Grandma all the time. His actual grandmothers are both in their seventies and she's only in her fifties.

In the closing scene of the book, the hesitant girl from the beginning page tells the story of how a stranger at the park asked her foster mother to "point out her real children." Her foster mother answered, "Oh, I don't have any imaginary children. All my children are real." The class erupts in laughter at this line. The read-aloud is over, but students are eager to talk more about their families.

The teacher decided to use this book to launch into a lesson that focuses on writing, speaking, and listening. A family tree is portrayed on one page of *A Family Is a Family Is a Family*, but Mrs. C has developed an alternative approach that does not focus on "sides" of the family or genetic links. She was motivated to diverge from that approach after exploring lessons on the Teaching Tolerance website (www.tolerance.org). Specifically, she adapted ideas from two lesson strands they have, including "My Family Rocks" and "Family Tapestry."

She starts the lesson with a scavenger hunt based on the book. Students are up and moving around the room trying to find peers who have families like the ones in the books as well as ones with other traits. Each student has to make three matches on the scavenger hunt list, which includes the following: find someone who lives with their grandparents, find an only child, find someone who has twins in their family, find someone who lives between two homes, and find someone whose family includes pets. After this step, students are paired up to interview each other about their families. When they are finished, they report to the class on one thing that's similar about their families and one thing that's different. Finally, students are given materials to write and draw about their own families. They can tell a story like in each page of *A Family Is a Family Is a Family*, or they can use a variation on a family tree, such as a map, wheel, flower garden, or a forest. Sources for these models include:

> www.familytreetemplates.net/category/nontraditional
> www.steampoweredfamily.com/education/modern-options-for-the-family-tree-project-that-promote-inclusiveness
> www.adoptionpolicy.org/Adoption_Awareness_Schools.pdf

Like *A Family Is a Family Is a Family*, the books in this chapter create opportunities for teachers to offer a more inclusive range of families in the literature they share. These multimodal activities and text sets offer rich and authentic portrayals of diverse families. The books in the first two sets focus on affirmation and appreciation, while the last set more directly addresses challenges families like these might face.

## MULTIMODAL TEXT SETS

### Text Set 1: Child-Centered Voice

This text set features books that demonstrate the power of a child's voice. The children in these books express pride in their family relationships or show the power they hold as a member of that family. Each book tells the story of a child insisting that their voices be heard as they present themselves honestly in the context of family or school life.

O'Leary, S. (2016). *A Family Is a Family Is a Family*. Ill. by Q. Leng. Toronto, Canada: Groundwood Books.

In the opening scene of this book, a child in a classroom is nervous when the teacher asks what makes their family special. She expresses this worry, saying, "My family is not like everybody else's." The book then continues with all the children in the class describing something special about their families. The voices of children in LGBTQ families, divorced families, stepfamilies, and those living with grandparents are heard. In the end, the child from the beginning reveals that she has a foster mother. The whimsical cartoon illustrations keep the mood of this story light, but the heart of the story is a child voicing pride in their family structure after initial hesitation.

Coffelt, N. (2007). *Fred Stays with Me.* Ill. by T. Tusa. New York, NY: Little, Brown & Company.

The young girl in this book describes her life living in two different homes. The sepia-toned pictures capture her life at her mom's house compared to life at her dad's house. The story is simple and straightforward as the protagonist describes the things her dog, Fred, does that bother her mom (barking at the dog next door) and her dad (stealing socks). When her parents try to tell her that Fred can't "stay" at their respective homes, she explains, "Fred doesn't stay with either of you. Fred stays with me." By taking this strong stance, she asserts herself and makes her role in the family clear. Her assertive personality is the heart of this story about a divorced family.

Averbeck, J. (2015). *One Word from Sophia.* Ill. by Y. Ismail. New York, NY: Antheneum Books.

In a purple tutu and ponytail, Sophia approaches her family with a plea for a giraffe for her birthday. While this premise may sound silly, Sophia has a clear plan to persuade her mother, father, uncle, and Grand-mama. Her mother and Grand-mama are brown-skinned like Sophia, while her father and uncle appear to be white. The illustrations are playful and messy with bursts of color. Sophia's self-confidence comes through as she asserts her arguments geared toward each family member. She is smart and determined in her approach to each family member. This book portrays a loved and confident child in a diverse family context.

Dufft, S. (2019). *Paula Knows What to Do.* Toronto, Canada: Pajama Press.

In this story, a young child is upset because her dad is sad and will not get out of bed; they both miss mommy. It is not clear what has happened to Paula's mother, just that she is "gone." Whether this story is about death, divorce, or another kind of loss, Paula comforts her parent through imaginative play. Much of the story is conveyed through art, which shifts the mood through the use of color and shadow. During the fantasy sequence, the art becomes childlike with bold brushstrokes, again keeping Paula at the center of the story. This parent and child are a family unit in the midst of the grieving process, but Paula is empowered and active in that process.

Friedman, D. (2009). *Star of the Week.* Ill. by R. Roth. New York, NY: HarperCollins.

In this adoption story, a kindergartener named Cassidy-Li must figure out how to talk about her family when she is "star of the week" at school. She knows she will make brownies with sprinkles, but she's not sure what she wants to put on the required poster. She knows she'll include a picture of her parents, friends, cousins, and pets, but what about her birth parents? Cassidy-Li was adopted from China and knows that "I am a part of them, and they are a part of me." This realistic story shows Cassidy-Li solving her own problem and negotiating sharing her family story with her class on her own terms.

Schiffer, M. (2015). *Stella Brings the Family*. Ill. by H. Clifton-Brown. San Francisco, CA: Chronicle Books.

In this school-based story, a young girl with two dads is worried about what she will do when her teacher explains that the class will hold a special Mother's Day party. The children are gathered on the rug, and Stella looks away from the circle, showing her panic and uneasiness. Her peers ask questions about what it is like not to have a mother, and Stella is able to answer each potentially hurtful wondering with confidence, but repeatedly says, "I have no mother to bring to the Mother's Day party." When the time comes to make the invitation, Stella comes up with the idea of inviting her extended family, which includes her Nonna, Aunt Gloria, and Cousin Lucy. This solution enables Stella to participate in the event and validates her family within the school context.

**Text Set 1: Multimodal Activities and Extensions**

Many of the characters in the books in this set have to make decisions about how to handle interactions with peers and adults as they negotiate family differences. This creates an opportunity for teachers to talk to children about how they respond emotionally to situations and the decision they have to make in order to assert their voice. Whitney (1999) proposes the idea of persona dolls as a way to help children think through how they or another child might be feeling. Persona dolls are used for a kind of storytelling as teachers assign the dolls identities and then invite children to explore what the dolls are feeling and experiencing. These dolls are kept separate from the dolls available for free play because they are used in a more direct way with teacher guidance. Examples can be found in *Anti-Bias Education* (Derman-Sparks & Edwards, 2010) and the Early Childhood Equity Alliance website. Best practice use of persona dolls incorporates another student into the classroom, one who has demographic differences that are not represented in the population. This opens up opportunities to help students think beyond themselves, building compassion and nurturing empathy.

In several of the books in this set, children have to speak up and out to adults. Paula coerces her dad to get out of bed even though he is sad; the young child in *Fred Stays with Me* demands that her dog remain with her, not at either of her parents' homes, Sophia knows what she wants and argues for her side. The protagonists in *A Family Is a Family Is a Family, Stella Brings the Family,* and *Star of the Week* all find confidence after initially worrying that their family would be viewed negatively. Teachers can be proactive in avoiding situations like this by focusing on inclusive language and projects that are flexible rather than based on assumptions about family types. The video *Our Family: A Film about Family Diversity* (www.niot.org/our-family-film-about-family-diversity) features seven minutes of testimonials from children from diverse families. The video was developed by Not in Our Town, a nonprofit organization dedicated to stopping hate and building inclusive communities. The teacher's guide offers pre- and post-viewing questioning strategies, discussion prompts, extension activities, as well as a "pause guide" with key moments that teachers can use to stop the film and ask questions, find out what the students are thinking and feeling, teach relevant vocabulary, or expand on information. Interactions like this can help students feel empowered and find their own voice.

**Text Set 2: Joy and Bonding**

The books in this set feature celebratory and joyous portrayals of families. The books are light-hearted in nature and highlight endearing connections between parents and children. Young readers will easily be able to see their own family interactions in the ones described in these titles. The mirrors provided in these books for children with these kinds of family structures are authentic and child centered.

Walsh, M. (2012). *Living with Mom and Living with Dad.* Somerville, MA: Candlewick Press.

In this inviting lift-the-flap book, a young girl describes how she spends her days living separately with her two parents. Sometimes she lives in a brick house with her mom and cat and other days in an apartment building with her dad. The little girl shares common pleasures that make her dual homes more accommodating, such as items from her satchel filled with shared toys and the events both parents attend. The brightly colored artwork is perfect for younger readers, and the pleasant and direct first-person narrator who takes a positive look at divorce normalizes and affirms the experience.

Woodson, J. (2002). *Visiting Day.* Ill. by J. Ransome. New York, NY: Scholastic.

In this beautifully illustrated picture book, a young African American girl travels with her grandmother to visit her father in prison. The story begins with the preparations both Grandma and the father make in the morning. The girl's voice narrates the day with the repetition of the phrase "only on visiting day." She wakes up smiling, shares food with friends on the bus ride, and then hugs and laughs with her father. She is sad after the visit but ultimately stays connected by making pictures to send her father and making plans with her grandmother for when he is home again. *Visiting Day* features a child living with a single grandparent and tells the story of an incarcerated parent without shame or embarrassment.

Alko, S. (2009). *I'm Your Peanut Butter Big Brother.* New York, NY: Alfred A. Knopf.

Told in lyrical prose with clever wordplay, this story involves a young boy wondering aloud what his new baby brother or sister will look like. As an interracial child, he wonders if the new baby will look like him or more like his "semisweet dark Daddy chocolate bar or strawberry cream mama's milk?" Throughout the text, food metaphors accompany the young boy's questions. The story is contextualized with a detailed author's note. Alko explains that she wrote the book based on her own wonderings when she was expecting her two children.

Bush, Z. (2018). *Made for Me.* Ill. by G. deLauretis. Sanger, CA: Familius.

This touching and simple rhyming book showcases the love and sense of belonging that a single father has for his young child. From the moment his son was born, the father is overcome with emotions as they bond. Told from his viewpoint, he exclaims: "On the day you were born, I beamed with pride. / My eyes filled with tears. I joyfully cried. / From the moment I saw you and called out your name, / the world as I knew it was never the same." This story in rhyme captures the joys of single fatherhood, and the endearing art makes it appealing to all families.

Levine, A. (2011). *Monday Is One Day.* Ill. by J. Hector. New York, NY: Scholastic.

This rhyming story cheerfully counts down the work week as a parent looks forward to weekend fun as a family. The diversity in this book includes a two-dad family, two single-parent families, and a child being raised on a farm by older caregivers. Scenes at breakfasts, bedtimes, and bus stops capture the little pleasures of weekday routines. The bright yellows and blues in the pictures will appeal to young children, along with the child-centered language. In the final pages of the book, all the families gather outdoors and watch the sunset.

Newman, L. (2009). *Daddy, Papa, and Me.* Ill. by C. Thompson. Berkeley, CA: Tricycle Press.

Newman, L. (2009). *Mommy, Mama, and Me.* Ill. by C. Thompson. Berkeley, CA: Tricycle Press.

These board books feature minimal text and short rhyming patterns. In each book, a young child describes interactions with their parents. In one, the child compares Mommy and Mama, while in the other Daddy and Papa are compared. In both books the child's love for their parents shines through. Each comparison is paired with a picture, so when "Papa helps me make a pie," the father and child are portrayed together doing the work of baking. Gender stereotypes are avoided as both dads do domestic tasks. The same pattern unfolds with the mothers, and the young child in both books is gender neutral. All of these features make for a playful and universal board book for the youngest readers.

**Text Set 2: Multimodal Activities and Extensions**

Teachers can help children build pride and confidence in their families by showing a film such as *That's a Family: A Film for Kids about Family Diversity* (Chasnoff, 2000), the purpose of which is to "not just learn about different families but to learn from different families." The Groundspark website (https://groundspark.org/our-films-and-campaigns/thatfamily) offers a wealth of resources to accompany the video, including a teaching guide, letters home, and links to further tools for inclusive schools. The Family Diversity Project (https://familydiv.org/about) offers a traveling exhibit that can be displayed in schools to visually show a range of families through photography. Schools, libraries, and other resource centers can collaborate to bring this show to their communities and may be inspired to create their own project featuring their community.

Using digital platforms such as Little Bird Tales (https://littlebirdtales.com) is an effective way for children to compose digital stories to celebrate their family structures and build respect for all families. It is important to invite and welcome families to the classroom to share family stories and to ensure that all children have the opportunity to discuss the important people in their lives. Adoption books can be easily incorporated into studies of community or family, which are common themes in early childhood curricula. For example, before or after reading *Happy Adoption Day* by John McCutcheon (1996), teachers can play the song performed by the author (www.youtube.com/watch?v=D3ZZtUe0l2Q). As young children explore the theme of family, it is important to develop strategies that help children understand the uniqueness of each family. The discussion of adoption works well, especially when helping young children to understand how each family is special, while still focusing on characteristics that all families share.

Teachers may need to rethink their "all about me" and traditional "Mother's/Father's Day" activities to be more inclusive. For example, instead of asking students to draw a picture of their house, they can direct students to draw a picture of their favorite possession and to draw pictures of the important people in their lives. In addition, teachers can incorporate an alternative family tree project to ensure that all children feel validated for their unique family structures. Some possible alternative family tree projects can be found at:

>www.familytreetemplates.net/category/nontraditional
>https://adoption.com/5-creative-family-trees-for-children-who-were-adopted
>www.adoptionpolicy.org/Adoption_Awareness_Schools.pdf

As teachers share the books in this text set, they will want to have open discussions about family structures. It is important to create an inviting environment and classroom community for students to feel comfortable to share information about themselves and the important people in their lives. Teachers can extend any of the books in the text set with videos, creative arts, writing, or digital storytelling. Using inclusive language and communication to ensure that all families are represented is an important component of instilling a sense of pride. There are some additional interactive activities and lessons on the Teaching Tolerance website (www.tolerance.org/lesson/my-family-journey) that will support the early childhood curriculum and to ensure that all families are valued.

## Text Set 3: Hope and Change

This text set highlights books for young readers that explore how characters find hope and resilience through transitions. Each selection provides readers with a well-written story that positions characters in challenging family scenarios. The characters face adversity and change but through family connections find positive responses and create understanding and connections.

Moundlic, C. (2011). *The Scar*. Ill. by O. Tallec. Somerville, MA: Candlewick Press.

Told through a young boy's perspective as he struggles with his feelings about his mother's death, this story shows sadness, despair, and anger. The boy worries about how his dad will know how to cut the toast like his mother did and he wonders if he will forget his mother, her smell, laugh, and stories. After scraping his knee, the young boy hears his mother's voice and decides not to bandage his scab. He told himself that "as long as there was blood, I would still hear my mom's voice." During a visit with his grandparents, he shares his fear that his mother's smell will disappear. His grandmother reassures him and says, "She's there, in your heart, and she's not going anywhere." The simple pencil illustrations and red-wash panels are poignant reminders that mirror the young boy's emotions from anger and fear to sadness and eventually acceptance.

Beaty, D. (2013). *Knock Knock: My Dad's Dream for Me.* Ill. by B. Collier. New York, NY: Little, Brown & Company.

In this poignant story, a young African American boy and his father share a morning ritual. A simple "Knock knock" on the door reminds the boy to be asleep or that he can wake up and jump in his father's arms. But, soon, the absence of the knocks and his father's presence cause extreme loneliness for the young boy. One day, the boy finds a letter from his father filled with words of both sadness and encouragement: "Knock Knock down the doors that I could not." Through this poignant note, the boy learns that his father will not return but that he has beautiful goals for him to live by. The collage illustrations create an urban landscape that enhance the emotional depth of the story. The author's note provides further explanation regarding the boy's missing father, adding to this story's power to encourage hope.

Woodson, J. (2002). *Our Gracie Aunt.* Ill. by J. Muth. New York, NY: Hyperion Books for Children.

In this beautifully written story, readers meet Johnson and his sister Beebee, two siblings who have become used to managing on their own when their mama disappears. Days pass and they try to avoid the social worker, who insists that they must stay with their Aunt Gracie. Even though she is a relative, she was a stranger to both Beebee and Johnson. Gradually the two children open their hearts to their Aunt Gracie, who reassures them that she will be their "Aunt Gracie for always." With masterful storytelling combined with soft illustrations, the emotional content of this story sends a powerful message to readers about finding courage and renewed hope.

Newman, L. (2011). *Donovan's Big Day.* Ill. by M. Dutton. Berkeley, CA: Tricycle Press.

Donovan starts his day knowing that he has "BIG" job to do. Even though there is a great deal of excitement in the house, Donovan still has to get ready and be careful to not make any extra messes. He has to zip up his jacket and remember to tuck the "little white satin box" to keep inside his pocket. As the story builds to the momentous celebration of the wedding of Donovan's two mothers, readers see Donovan overcoming his trepidations of falling or tripping on the way to the church. This beautiful occasion is marked by Donovan presenting his Mother and Mama the gold rings and celebrating his joy by giving his moms a huge hug and kiss, which marks a new family beginning.

Heo, Y. (2009). *Ten Days and Nine Nights: An Adoption Story.* New York, NY: Random House.

This endearing story about an international adoption will pique the interest of readers with the inclusion of an interactive countdown calendar. The narrator, a young girl, marks down each of the ten days and nine nights on her calendar until the arrival of her new sister from Korea. Throughout the story, brightly colored illustrations and wordless panels show an extended family working together to prepare for their new arrival. While the little girl practices holding and feeding a baby with a doll, other members of her family are preparing for the big day. Her grandmother sews a new outfit, her parents assemble a crib and complete the adoption paperwork, and the little girl washes a teddy bear. As the entire family leaves for the airport to meet their new baby, everyone is joyful and eager for this positive life change.

**Text Set 3: Multimodal Activities and Extensions**

Teachers can support children as they cope with life transitions through dialogue, dramatic play, and writing. Students who experience a loss or disruption to their family structure need opportunities to talk about their feelings. Establishing a safe classroom atmosphere will foster resilience, coping skills, and the ability to find courage. Students who are coping with a loss or a life transition may find it helpful to write/draw on a white board or other device. They can record their feelings using AudioBoo or Flipgrid. These tools allow children to keep their stories private or share when they are ready or only with those they are comfortable with.
Links:

AudioBoo: www.appsinclass.com/audioboo.html
Flipgrid: https://flipgrid.com

Another strategy to assist students is to create a memory box. Students place objects, pictures, cards, and other items about a loved one that are particularly significant. Students would be encouraged to talk about the objects or to use the objects as a springboard for writing. Another idea is to invite students to compose a memory book or collage. Students can use traditional modes of creating a collage or experiment with digital tools such as PicCollage for Kids. Teachers will want to impress upon students that the final products can be for the private settings, but when students are ready, they may bring in the memory box to share with a school counselor or even with a group of friends. Teachers may also want to co-plan lessons with grief counselors and members of the school community.
Links:

Memory Box: https://sesamestreetformilitaryfamilies.org/topic/grief/?ytid=sE3aWr6Mc7s
https://familydiv.org

PicCollage for Kids: https://itunes.apple.com/ca/app/pic-collage-for-kids-best/id977081997?mt=8&ign-mpt=uo%3D4

Teachers can also adapt Georgia Heard's (2016) heart maps, which provides students with authentic writing opportunities and the freedom to explore their feelings and ideas. The heart maps also have the capacity for all students to empathize with others and to launch meaningful conversations about their lives. Teachers can also adapt Susan Van Zile and colleagues' (2012) simile portrait writing extension about someone special. In this activity, students write down special characteristics, memories, and loving words about one person.

In addition, teachers may want to adapt the "I am" or "Bio Poem" templates to provide students with another outlet to express their feelings.

Links:

Heart Map: www.georgiaheard.com/heart-maps

Simile Portrait: www.scholastic.com/teachers/books/using-picture-books-to-teach-8-essential-literary-elements-by-em

I am Poem: www.readwritethink.org/files/resources/lesson_images/lesson391/I-am-poem.pdf

Bio Poem: www.readwritethink.org/files/resources/lesson_images/lesson398/biopoem.pdf

## ADDITIONAL RECOMMENDED BOOKS ABOUT FAMILY

Ada, A. F. (2002). *I Love Saturdays y Domingos*. Ill. by E. Savadier. New York, NY: Antheneum Books for Young Readers.

Birtha, B. (2017). *Far Apart, Close in Heart*. Chicago, IL: Albert Whitman.

Brown, L. (2016). *The Airport Book*. New York, NY: Roaring Brook Press.

Daly, C. (2014). *Emily's Blue Period*. Ill. by L. Brown. New York, NY: Roaring Brook Press.

DiPucchio, K. (2019). *Littles and How They Grow*. New York, NY: Doubleday Books for Young Readers.

Eagan, K. (2012). *Kate and Nate Are Running Late*. Ill. by D. Yaccarino. New York, NY: Feiwel & Friends.

Harris, R. (2012). *Who's in My Family?* Ill. by N. Westcott. Somerville, MA: Candlewick Press.

Hoffman, M. (2011). *The Great Big Book of Families*. New York, NY: Dial Books.

Holmberg, B. (2008). *Day with Dad*. Ill. by E. Eriksson. Somerville, MA: Candlewick Press.

Isadora, R. (2006). *What Is a Family? A Fresh Look at Family Trees*. New York, NY: Putnam.

Juster, N. (2005). *The Hello Goodbye Window*. Ill. by C. Raschka. New York, NY: Hyperion Books for Children.

Kuklin, S. (2006). *Families*. New York, NY: Hyperion Books for Children.

Lunde, S. (2013). *My Father's Arms Are a Boat*. New York, NY: Enchanted Lion Books.

MacLachlan, P. (2013). *You Were the First*. Ill. by S. Graegin. New York, NY: Little, Brown and Company.

Mallery, S. (2018). *A Most Unusual Day*. Ill. by E. B. Goodale. New York, NY: HarperCollins Publishing.

Monk, Isabell. (2001). *Family*. Minneapolis, MN: Carolrhoda Books.

Nahr, S. (2019). *Maisie's Scrapbook.* Ill. by J. Loring-Fisher. London, UK: Lantana Books Ltd.
Oelschlager, V. (2010). *A Tale of Two Daddies.* Ill by M. Blanc. Akron, OH: Vanita Books.
Oelschlager, V. (2011). *A Tale of Two Mommies.* Ill by K. Blackwood & M. Blanc. Akron, OH: Vanita Books.
Rocco, J. (2011). *Blackout.* New York, NY: Disney-Hyperion Books.
Rotner, S. (2011). *I'm Adopted!* New York, NY: Holiday House.
Rotner, S. (2015). *Families.* Photos by S. Kelly. New York, NY: Holiday House.
Schiffer, M. (2018). *Stella Brings the Family.* Ill. by H. Clifton-Brown. San Francisco, CA: Chronicle Books.
Shannon, G. (2015). *One Family.* Ill. by B. Gomez. New York, NY: Frances Foster Books/ Farrar, Straus & Giroux.
Sima, J. (2018). *Harriet Gets Carried Away.* New York, NY: Simon and Schuster.
Smet, M. (2012). *I Have Two Homes.* Ill. by N. Talsma. New York, NY: Clavis.
Stansbie, S. (2018). *My Friends and Me.* Ill. by K. Halford. Wilton, CT: Tiger Tales.
Stanton, K. (2014). *Monday, Wednesday, and Every Other Weekend.* New York, NY: Feiwel & Friends.
Woodson, J. (2010). *Pecan Pie Baby.* Ill. by S. Blackall. New York, NY: G.P. Putnam's Sons.
Young, E. (2006). *My Mei Mei.* New York, NY: Philomel/Penguin.

## AUTHOR SPOTLIGHT: INTERVIEW WITH LESLEA NEWMAN

Leslea Newman is a groundbreaking writer for readers of all ages. She may be best known for her 1989 book *Heather Has Two Mommies*, which was a breakthrough book because of its representation of an LGBTQ family. Newman has gone on to publish everything from board books to teen novels. She has garnered a range of awards including the Stonewall Book Award, the Lambda Literary Award, the Amelia Bloomer Award (now called Rise: A Feminist Book Project), and the Sydney Taylor Award. Her books focus on families with an emphasis on LGBTQ and Jewish themes, but she also publishes poetry, magazines articles, and anthologies. Some of her most renowned books include *October Mourning: A Song for Matthew Shepard* (2012), *Hachiko Waits* (2009), and *Sparkle Boy* (2017).

*1. Please share your thinking about the importance of multicultural literature in the early childhood classroom.*

The world is diverse; the literature in every child's class should be diverse as well. As Dr. Rudine Sims Bishop states, children need books that are mirrors and windows: mirrors so that they can see themselves reflected, which makes them feel validated and know they have a place in this world; windows so they can look out and learn about others and thereby develop compassion.

*2. Some multicultural books affirm and explore identity. Explain how you do this in your books.*

By writing about all types of families, including two-mom families, two-dad families, single-parent families, as well as books about gender-creative and gender-free children, I give many different types of readers the opportunity to see themselves in literature (affirm) and see others in literature (explore). My hope is to "change the world one book at a time" and help create a world of people who are respectful, accepting, and able to celebrate everyone.

*3. Select one of your favorite books or poems, and share how you would explore it with young learners.*

I would read my book *Sparkle Boy* to young readers, which has many pauses built into the text where the adult reader can ask the young learners what they think. Casey likes to wear sparkly skirts, nail polish, and bracelets just like his big sister Jessie. When he says to his mother, after seeing Jessie in a shimmery skirt, "Ooh. I want shimmery," the text says, "Casey's mother thought for a minute." One can ask young listeners, "What do you think Casey's mother is thinking? What are you thinking?" This goes on all throughout the text, giving listeners a chance to think for themselves.

*4. What advice would you give early childhood teachers as they attempt to explore concepts of identity with young children through multicultural literature.*

I would advise teachers to first look inside themselves and really be honest with how you feel about these issues. Children can sense discomfort and unease. Make sure you do your own internal homework before discussing these issues in your classroom.

*5. What classroom suggestions can you provide for teachers to select and incorporate diverse books into their curriculum?*

I suggest a visit to We Need Diverse Books, which has all types of resources: https://diversebooks.org.

*6. What are your hopes and dreams for early childhood classrooms and libraries in the future?*

To be filled with books that show as many different families and identities as possible so that all children find themselves represented in books in a positive way.

*7. Some teachers are hesitant to talk about diversity with young children. What words of encouragement can you offer them?*

It is absolutely crucial to have a diverse library in your classroom. I can't state this strongly enough. Children are not born with preconceived notions about who belongs in a family or what type of gender expression is acceptable. Unfortunately, sometimes they internalize bigoted messages from the adults around them who are not accepting and respectful of all people. Once this is learned, it can be difficult or confusing to unlearn. Making a safe space in your classroom where all children of all backgrounds, family constellations, and identities feel welcome can and does save lives. There is nothing more important than teaching children to be empathetic, compassionate, and kind.

## REFERENCES

Adoption Network. (n.d.). Adoption Statistics. Retrieved from https://adoptionnetwork.com/adoption-statistics

Baxley, T. P. (2008). "What are you?" Biracial children in the classroom. *Childhood Education, 84*(4), 230–233.

Chasnoff, D. (Director). (2000). *That's a Family!* [Film]. Groundspark.

Chaudhri, A. (2017). *Multiracial identity in children's literature.* New York, NY: Routledge.

Cherlin, A. (2010). Demographic trends in the United States: A review of research in the 2000s. *Journal of Marriage and Family, 72*(3), 403–419.

Child Welfare Information Gateway. (2011). How many children were adopted in 2007 and 2008? Retrieved from www.childwelfare.gov/pubs/adopted0708

Child Welfare Information Gateway. (2016). *Trends in U.S. adoptions: 2008–2012.* Retrieved from www.childwelfare.gov/pubs/adopted0812

Copenhaver-Johnson, J., Bowman, J., & Rietschlin, A. J. (2008). Culturally responsive read-alouds in first grade: Drawing upon children's languages and cultures to facilitate literary and social understandings. In J. C. Scott, D. Y. Straker, & L. Katz (Eds.), *Affirming students' right to their own languages: Bridging language policies and pedagogical practices* (pp. 206–218). New York, NY: Routledge.

Corr, C. (2003–2004). Bereavement, grief, and mourning in death-related literature for children. *OMEGA—Journal of Death and Dying, 48*(4), 337–363.

Corr, C. (2010). A book on the death of a pet: To be read by or with a child. *Death Studies, 34*(10), 955–957.

Crenshaw, K. (1989). Demarginalizing the intersection of race and sex: A black feminist critique of antidiscrimination doctrine, feminist theory and antiracist politics. *University of Chicago Legal Forum, 1989*(1), article 8.

Derman-Sparks, L., & Edwards, J. O. (2010). *Anti-bias education for young children and ourselves* (2nd ed.). Washington, DC: National Association for the Education of Young Children.

Dutro, E. (2008). That's why I was crying on this book: Trauma as testimony in children's responses to literature. *Changing English, 15*(4), 423–434.

Evans-Santiago, B., & Lin, M. (2016). Preschool through grade 3: Inclusion with sensitivity: Teaching children with LGBTQ families. *YC Young Children, 71*(2), 56–63.

Gadja, R. (2004). Responding to the needs of the adopted child. *Kappa Delta Pi Record, 40*(4), 160–164.

Gates, G. J. (2013). *LGBT parenting in the United States.* The Williams Institute. Retrieved from http://williamsinstitute.law.ucla.edu/wp-content/uploads/LGBT-Parenting.pdf

Greenberg, J. (2001). "She is so my real mom!" Helping children understand adoption as one form of family diversity. *Young Children, 56*(2), 90–91.

Heard, G. (2016). *Heart maps: Helping students to create and craft authentic writing.* Portsmouth, NH: Heinemann.

"Intersectionality." (n.d.). *Oxford English Dictionary.* Retrieved from www.oed.com/view/Entry/429843

Kreider, R. (2011). Living arrangements of children: 2009, Current population reports, U.S. Census Bureau, Washington, DC. Retrieved from www.census.gov/prod/2011pubs/p70-126.pdf

Lee, J., & Bean, F. D. (2012). A postracial society or a diversity paradox? *Du Bois Review, 9*(2), 419–437.

Livingston, G. (2015). Today's multiracial babies reflect America's changing demographics. Washington, DC: Pew Research Center. Retrieved from www.pewresearch.org/fact-tank/2015/06/24/todays-multiracial-babies-reflect-americas-changing-demographics

Murphy, D., & Cooper, P. M. (2015). Parents behind bars: What happens to their children? Washington, DC: *Child Trends*. Retrieved from www.childtrends.org/wp-content/uploads/2015/10/2015-42ParentsBehindBars.pdf

National Association for the Education of Young Children. (2005). "The ten NAEYC program standards." Retrieved from www.naeyc.org/our-work/families/10-naeyc-program-standards

National Association for the Education of Young Children. (2010). Standards for initial and advanced early childhood professional preparation programs. Retrieved from www.naeyc.org/sites/default/files/globally-shared/downloads/PDFs/our-work/higher-ed/NAEYC-Professional-Preparation-Standards.pdf

Nesmith, A., & Ruhland, E. (2008). Children of incarcerated parents: Challenges and resiliency, in their own words. *Children and Youth Services Review, 30*(10), 1119–1130.

Polak, M. (2007, October). The road to recovery. *National Post.*

Scanlon-McMath, J., & King, M. (2011). Biracial/multiracial children and families in picture books. *International Journal of the Book, 8*(3), 157–164.

Short, K. G. (2011). Reading literature in elementary classrooms. In S. A. Wolf, K. Coats, P. Enciso, & C. Jenkins (Eds.), *Handbook of research on children's and young adult literature* (pp. 48–62). New York, NY: Routledge.

Simmons, T., & Dye, J. L. (2003). Grandparents living with children. U.S. Census Bureau. Retrieved from www.census.gov/prod/2003pubs/c2kbr-31.pdf

Smith-D'Arezzo, W. M. (2018). Supporting adopted children and their families: Using picture books to tell the stories of adoption. *Young Children, 73*(4), 28–34.

U.S. Census Bureau. (2016, November 17). Majority of children live with two parents, Census Bureau reports. Retrieved from www.census.gov/newsroom/press-releases/2016/cb16-192.html

U.S. Census Bureau. (2018, January 19). More children live with just their fathers than a decade ago. Retrieved from www.census.gov/newsroom/press-releases/2017/living-arrangements.html

Van Zile, S., Napoli, M., & Ritholz, E. (2012). *Literary elements toolkit for grades 4–8*. New York, NY: Scholastic.

Wardle, F., & Cruz-Janzen, M. I. (2004). *Meeting the needs of multiethnic and multiracial children in school.* Boston, MA: Pearson Education.

Whitney, T. (1999). *Kids like us: Using persona dolls in the classroom.* St. Paul, MN: Redleaf Press.

Wildeman, C., Haskins, A., & Poehlmann-Tynan, J. (2018). *When parents are incarcerated: Interdisciplinary research and interventions to support children.* Washington, DC: American Psychological Association.

## Additional Children's Literature Cited

Engel, C. (2017). *Baby's first words.* Cambridge, MA: Barefoot Books.
Lang, S., & Lang, M. (2015). *Families families families.* New York, NY: Random House.
Maclear, K. (2010). *Spork.* Toronto: Kids Can Press.
Newman, L. (1989). *Heather has two mommies.* New York, NY: Alyson Books.
O'Leary, S. (2016). *A Family Is a Family Is a Family.* Ill. by Q. Leng. Toronto, Canada: Groundwood Books.
Parr, T. (2003). *The family book.* New York, NY: Little, Brown Books for Young Readers.
Richardson, J., & Parnell, P. (2005). *And Tango makes three.* Ill. by H. Cole. New York, NY: Simon & Schuster.

*Chapter Three*

# Partnering at School

## Being Friends

- In what ways can teachers foster conversations about friendships among classmates and assist students in building relationships with similar and dissimilar peers?
- How can early childhood teachers infuse literature to promote kindness, connections, and self-regulation using friendship-based stories?
- How can early childhood classrooms incorporate literature that encourages each child's sense of individual worth and belonging as a part of a classroom community?

Building friendships is a vital component in the social and emotional development of young children. Literature with themes of friendship can foster conversations about positive ways to interact with peers in school settings. By using high-quality literature focused on stories of friendship, teachers can help children resolve conflicts, raise consciousness, identify their feelings, and explore ways to bridge differences.

Chris Raschka's (1993) groundbreaking book *Yo? Yes!* portrays an emerging friendship between two boys with distinct physical differences. The book won the Caldecott Medal and is highly regarded as a deceptively simple book with immense teaching potential. *Yo? Yes!* highlights the complex dynamics of friendship among young people. Through minimal dialogue and the use of body language, the two boys in the book try to figure out how and if they can be friends. The book captures the realities of how complicated peer interactions can be for young children.

While there may be a societal romanticization of children as innocent, colorblind, and easily able to make friends, research shows that the interactions are far more complex. Children need books that realistically portray the joys and challenges of cross-cultural friendships and help them think about how to build compassion and support peers who may be marginalized because of differences.

Early childhood educators may be familiar with some titles that have endured over time, such as *Will I Have a Friend* (Cohen, 1967/2009), *Swimmy* (Lionni, 1963), and *Marianthe's Story: Painted Words* (Aliki, 1998). These books have lasted because of how they continue to resonate with young children. Even though these books were published before the current focus on bullying and social anxiety among children, they speak to these concerns beneath the surface. A quick internet search gleans multiple long lists of best books for friendships and the first day of school.

These books are often appealing because they bring humor and imagination to the reading experience. Books by Caldecott winner Kevin Henkes such as *Owen* (1993) and *Chrysanthemum* (1991) are beloved by teachers and address the emotional challenges of going to school. Other popular fantasy stories of this nature include *Stick and Stone* (Ferry, 2015), *Hooway for Wodney Wat* (Lester, 1999), *The Kissing Hand* (Penn, 1993), and the Miss Bindergarten books (Slate, 1996). The vast number of books about making friends and starting school shows the enduring relevance of this topic.

The books selected for this chapter are recently published high-quality books that feature diverse characters. Popular books such as *How Full Is Your Bucket?* (Rath & Reckmeyer, 2009) or *The Rainbow Fish* (Pfister, 1992) offer idealized easy answers and attempt to overtly teach the value of friendship. Alternatively, the recommended titles have the potential to help early childhood teachers as they guide children through the real-life challenges of their social worlds.

According to NAEYC's Early Learning Program Accreditation Standards (2018), children need opportunities to foster healthy social and emotional growth through the development of friendships, self-regulation skills, empathy, and the ability to resolve conflicts in positive ways. Friendships, both in and out of school, are an integral part of a child's life. As early as age four, 75 percent of children in group settings are observed having frequent, reciprocal, cooperative, positive interactions with selected peers (Howes, 1996).

The question of how those peers are selected is crucial to this chapter. Friendship and its definitions have been the focus of research since the 1930s (Gronlund, 1959; Moreno, 1934; Carter & Nutbrown, 2016). Friendship is about "liking" one another and "liking" spending time together (Bukowski et al., 1996). Friendships are voluntary, intimate, dynamic relationships founded on cooperation and trust. They often depend on group acceptance perceptions of the child's peer group (Gifford-Smith & Brownwell, 2003, p. 248).

Since the features and significance of friendship vary greatly according to the stage of a child's social development (Dunn, 2004, p. 13), it is important that early childhood educators understand the ways friendships are formed and select books than can help guide children in their efforts. Sociological perspectives focus on how children construct their own peer culture (Bagwell & Schmidt, 2011) and how friendship functions for children in groups. Accordingly, teachers need to work to learn about the "peer culture" of the classroom and then demonstrate the value of friendship and make time and space for friendship (Carter & Nutbrown, 2016).

Helping children navigate peer interactions is not as simple as reminding the class that "we are all friends." The phrase "we are all friends" is widely embraced in early childhood classrooms (Wohlwend, 2007; Watson, 2018). Holding this basic idea of communal connections may seem ideal, but it provides little practical help to teachers trying to create inclusive classrooms or to the children in those classrooms. The similar phase "everyone is welcome" in the classroom fails to acknowledge the specific reasons or differences that might make someone not feel welcome. These simple phrases will not lead to positive efforts unless educators "can hear, recognize and challenge conversations among children, and among educators and children, which recreate the norm and the status quo" (Wohlwend, 2007, p. 10).

The focus on a kind of idealized and colorblind approach to classroom community building does not equip children with the skills or motivation to build friendships across differences. Sharing picture books that directly tell stories of children's experiences of exclusion for specific reasons will open dialogue between teachers and children about how their social world works and how friendships can be forged and maintained.

## THE REALITIES OF CHILDREN'S FRIENDSHIPS

Some children enter school with social experience and practice being with peers and making friends. They may have attended daycare, preschool, or other kinds of programming through libraries, churches, and community centers. Early childhood educators and parents recognize the importance of positive social interactions as they model how to greet each other, share toys, and express concerns about those around them. According to Smith-Bonahue et al. (2015), "One of the most important teaching tasks for early educators is helping children learn how to engage positively with peers" (p. 81).

However, outside of social-emotional learning theory, there is not an adequate focus in teacher preparation or professional development on how and why we foster friendships in the classroom. Teachers want to prevent bullying and empower children to form healthy and lasting friendships, and research shows that "having a friend seems to function as a protective factor for those children who are at risk of problems with peer groups" (Rubin et al., 2008, p. 1087). The books featured in this chapter offer stories of children who are insiders and outsiders as they navigate peer relationships and form social alliances.

Teachers and researchers recognize a range of benefits of friendships in childhood, such as "fun, emotional security, helpfulness, and validation of interests" (Rubin et al., 2008, p. 1086). These are just a few of the reasons that friendship is beneficial, but teachers need to know more about how to help children navigate making friends and maximize these relationships on the interpersonal level and for the greater good.

Research shows that from a very young age, children form friendships with peers who are similar to them or that friendships may be based on complementary needs or reciprocity (Parsons, 1996; Rubin et al., 2008; Aboud et al., 2003). Clearly, children's friendships are not simple, natural, or easy. Studies of young children's friendship show that they are aware of liability or social acceptance by other group members, their salience or dominance in groups, and how they are perceived by peers (Hawley, 2002; Hymel et al., 1993; Hymel & Swearer, 2015; Hartup, 1996).

This correlates with the fact that young children are "aware of diversity and difference from an early age and are capable of identifying what they understand as the normalized or the right way to be" (Robinson & Jones-Diaz, 2005, p. 41). We also know that during early childhood, children are beginning to develop in-group and out-group identities and apply emerging moral principles, such as fairness and equality, to their conceptualizations of these groups (Rutland et al., 2010). Similarity as a reason for forming friendship is evidenced across the research (Aboud et al., 2003; Crystal et al., 2008).

It is certainly a source of joy when children find peers with shared interests or shared backgrounds, including racial or cultural commonalities. Children may be drawn to similarity as well as to the advantages earned by certain friendships, but teachers and caregivers can cultivate a classroom culture that nurtures friendships that expand beyond social categories and offer interactions across differences.

Studies of childhood friendship patterns have failed to focus on cross-race or cross-cultural friendships. Regardless of the size of a children's friend group or the degree of intimacy within friendships, all of these relationships provide a "window into the thoughts, feelings, and desires of another" (Fink & Hughes, 2019, p. 28). Cross-race friendships are associated with both prejudice reduction and social and academic strengths (Crystal et al., 2008; Newgent et al., 2007).

According to Gaias et al. (2019), cross-race friendship contributes significantly to a reduction in future racial bias and calls on teachers to "intentionally facilitate these friendships among young children" (p. 13). Their study indicated a need for ongoing exposure to and interaction with diversity, rather than limited or generalized experienced. Indeed, according to this study, the sharing of the kinds of books featured in this chapter will not be adequate for cultivating enduring and authentic cross-race or otherwise heterogeneous friendships. Pettigrew (1998) argues that the best way to change negative attitudes and stereotypes is through interactions with individuals from different racial and ethnic groups.

This is a lofty goal, especially for highly segregated or culturally homogenous classroom settings. Diverse books that portray cross-cultural interactions have the potential to be a powerful tool in this endeavor. For the purposes of this chapter, cross-cultural friendships can include not only interactions across racial, ethnic, and cultural differences but also alliances built across other kinds of differences such as disability, socioeconomic status, and gender performance.

One teacher committed to providing opportunities for students to think critically about how markers related to socioeconomic status shaped peer interactions within the classroom community is showcased in the following vignette.

## CLASSROOM VIGNETTE: *EACH KINDNESS*

On a beautiful spring day, the first and second grade students in Mrs. H.'s multiage class gathered as a community for the shared reading of *Each Kindness* (2012), written by Jacqueline Woodson and illustrated by E. B. Lewis. Before reading the text, Mrs. H. asked her class to examine the cover and make predictions. After sharing this powerful story with her class, Mrs. H. reported the following:

> One of my students in my class is a twin. He and his brother have experienced a lot in their short lives; he, in particular, is less naïve and trusting than many in his age bracket. In most cases, he holds a glass-half-empty view of the world. He was very vocal about this book—he identified with Maya quickly. About halfway through, he stated that all children's books are unrealistic and have happy endings, so this one would, too. He seemed to have a kinship with the plot but with a sense of distrust at where it was leading, afraid that it would greatly disappoint him.
>
> When I finished reading, most of the students were silent, seemingly shocked and processing the book's implications. However, this student seemed to rise with fortification. He championed the book right away, and still does. It was encouraging to see him positively surprised by a book and to see him spreading this crucial message for his classmates to catch on to.
>
> It was interesting to witness the different ways that my students processed Maya's situation and how she should be treated. Many of my students are aware that I like to shop at places like Community Aid, so at first, they likened

Maya to their teacher when they realized she was wearing secondhand clothing. They thought that was "cool" and did not initially see it as a sign of poverty.

Peer pressure and social drama start so young, and my students quickly recognized and identified these social situations. However, they were indignant that Chloe wouldn't smile or include Maya. Their frustration built as Chloe's unkindness continued. The things that Maya played with and held out to show the others were things that my kids found fun, and they didn't understand why the other characters wouldn't want to play with them (or Maya).

Most of my students did not see Chloe as a mean girl, but rather as someone with similar experiences who kept making the wrong choices but surely would start making the right ones. When Maya's seat was empty, the kids kept thinking that she would be coming back soon. They were sure that Chloe would have a second chance to make things better with Maya.

The end of the book was a lot for most of my kids to process. They showed anger and frustration for Maya and the students in the class who should have been kinder to her. They were worried about Maya and where she went after Chloe's school. Was she okay? Did she have a place to live and enough to eat? Were her new classmates nice to her at the new school?

The idea that an act of kindness can have ripple effects was something that my students had to work on over time. Some of my students thought that they did not do enough kind acts themselves and took a while to really realize that they do not always think about the daily kindnesses that they perform. They initially struggled with thinking of potential ripple effects from one act of kindness, as these effects are not always seen by the initiator.

After a few days, however, my students were in the groove. They began to point out acts of kindness and imagine what power they may have on others. They began to be more deliberate, too, in their actions. They have been more other-oriented and intentional, and they link it to this book, as some literally say, "Remember, each kindness has power!"

After reading the book, Mrs. H. indicated that her class conducted many conversations about the overarching themes. The class continued to embrace the theme of kindness, and Mrs. H. indicated that this book would become a staple in her school-wide efforts to foster empathy. She also extended the book in various ways. First, she invited her class to replicate the scene from the story where Chloe's teacher demonstrates how a stone makes ripples in the water, just as one kindness has its ripple effects in the world. Then, she provided students with the opportunity to role-play potential situations and explore ways kindness could change things for the better. Though many of Mrs. H.'s students were already exhibiting kindness, she challenged her class to be intentional with their acts of kindness.

As displayed in figure 3.1, the students created their own kindness ripples, where they wrote one act of kindness that they could do for someone else in the center. They then imagined a possible outcome of that kind act and wrote that on the neighboring ring. On each subsequent ring, they wrote a possible effect of the previous ring, demonstrating the compounding effect kindness can have on the world.

The text sets developed for "partnering at school" include books that have the potential to nurture empathy. All books meet the following criteria: copyright dates after 2000, readily available in school and public libraries, strong literary quality rather than simplistic or didactic themes, and diverse characters or settings. The first text set includes books and activities that focus on the first day of school and being welcomed into new social contexts, while the second set addresses challenges and conflicts that may arise around friendships.

Figure 3.1. Student Writing Sample

# Chapter 3

## MULTIMODAL TEXT SETS

### Text Set 1: Facing Firsts and Taking Risks

This text set includes books that encourage excitement about entering school and making friends. The characters are nervous about transitioning to school, meeting peers, and finding their place in the classroom community. Some of the children are resistant and vocal about not wanting to go to school, while others are just hesitant or underconfident. As a set, the books explore the roles of parents, teachers, and peers in the process of adjusting to school and making social connections.

Yum, H. (2012). *Mom, It's My First Day of Kindergarten*. New York, NY: Frances Foster Books.

The young child in this book is excited for school, but his mom is worried. This role reversal makes the book unique and highly child-centered. The mom is portrayed as tiny and blue as the boy gets ready for school, but once they are at school, the boy begins to turn small and blue, demonstrating his fear and anxiety. After meeting his teacher, making friends, and getting to work, he thinks that kindergarten is "awesome," and he feels "so much bigger." Toward the end of the book, a double-page spread shows a row of parents waiting to pick up their children, including two fathers and a woman with a head covering.

Calabrese, K. (2018). *Lena's Shoes Are Nervous*. Ill. by J. Medina. New York, NY: Antheneum.

The playful illustrations, bold type, and child-centered tone make this an ideal book for talking about challenges related to the first day of school. Lena tells her dad that she's excited for school but explains that her shoes are nervous. Her dad joyfully engages with Lena, asking if her dress or headband "with the bright green flower" can help her shoes feel better. The relationship between father and daughter is the focus as much as the tensions around starting school. This is further emphasized through the art which uses white backgrounds but characters in full color. Lena appears to have a single dad, and the two have distinctly different skin tones. When the family approaches the school, they encounter diverse classmates, including a child using a wheelchair and a girl wearing a hijab.

Barnes, D. (2019). *The King of Kindergarten*. Ill. by V. Brantley-Newton. New York, NY: Nancy Paulsen Books

The young African American protagonist in this book taps into his confidence and excitement about school by thinking of himself as royalty. As he enters the school building, he sees his reflection in the windows with a chalk crown on his head. The school bus is described as "a big yellow carriage," and he pretends to battle a "fire-breathing dragon." His teacher is African American, and the class is highly diverse. The boy makes friends in class, on the playground, and in the lunchroom. This is a colorful, affirming, and celebratory book about becoming a part of a new classroom community.

Woodson, J. (2018). *The Day You Begin*. Ill. by R. López. New York, NY: Nancy Paulsen Books.

Sometimes a child's first day in a classroom is marked by fear and hesitation because they are new to the community. *The Day You Begin* captures the perspective of students who enter a classroom and feel like "no one there is quite like you." The characters are nervous about how they look (skin, clothes, hair) but also about their language, lunches, and even their summer vacations. The rich acrylic illustrations evoke nature and focus on facial expressions to capture the emotions of the characters. The story portrays subtle forms of bullying as well as more direct kinds of exclusion. In the end, the main character, Angelina, makes friends with Rigoberto, who recently moved from Venezuela. This book addresses the ways children might feel like outsiders in the classroom, on the first day of school, or any day of the year.

## Text Set 1: Multimodal Activities and Extensions

One way to integrate these books into the classroom is to use them as a point of entry to discuss classroom expectations. Conventional practices for setting up classroom routines and practices often neglect student voice and perspectives. Since it is clear from these texts that students are anxious about school for a variety of reasons, it is important that teachers find ways to help children unpack those feelings and strategize ways to minimize their effect. One way to do this is by co-creating classroom "guidelines" rather than rules.

When children are empowered to create standards for classroom interactions and behavior, they will be complying with their own guidelines rather than someone else's expectations and have a greater sense of ownership. Goularte (2000) explains that "giving students the opportunity to provide input on classroom goals and expectations helps them become productive participants in community building and may help increase their intellectual as well as social development" (p. 2).

Another way to make the first day of school easier and to help new students adjust throughout the year is a "kindness exchange" (King, 2017). Teachers can use a digital wall through tools like Padlet, Corkulous, or Google Docs or use sticky notes on poster paper to encourage children to notice acts of kindness as they happen around them. Every time they observe an act of kindness, they can add it to the wall through words or drawings. These notes would be anonymous, and the teacher can decide when or how to highlight the items that made it to the wall. These notes can encourage kindness through peer interaction, not just through teacher encouragement and modeling. In many classrooms, teachers encourage acts of kindness by directing kindness assignments themselves. One local teacher assigns students special agent names. She delivers envelopes with secret kindness instructions to all of her agents. One instruction might invite a student to write an anonymous note of encouragement to a student having difficulty with a subject, while another agent could receive instructions to do some extra cleaning to surprise the janitor. Students jump at the chance to covertly deliver their acts of kindness.

Early childhood educators will want to be proactive and preventive in their efforts to support children in their friendships and social interactions. One way to do this is to share scenarios that may challenge children before they happen. Incorporating podcasts into the classroom routine can offer opportunities for dialogue and reflection. *Short and Curly* (www.abc.net.au/radio/programs/shortandcurly) is a podcast available through ABC radio and in partnership with the Ethics Centre. The podcast is dedicated to helping young people navigate the ethics of relationships. One of the goals is to help children as they are "finding out who we are and staying true to that in the face of temptations, challenges and uncertainty." Recent episodes include "When Should You Stop Being Friends with Someone?" and "How to Make the Best Kinds of Friends." The episodes are approximately twenty minutes and add humor and silliness as they grapple with these tough questions that will help children think about the choices they would make in similar situations.

Another resource for teachers to help children manage their feelings and choices in relationships is the podcast *Peace Out* (https://bedtime.fm/peaceout). This podcast has a shorter running time of usually less than fifteen minutes and is somewhat designed for bedtime. However, *Peace Out* is ideal for a rest time in a preschool or after-recess regrouping in elementary school settings. One episode titled "Reflect, Respect, and Connect" asks listeners to consider how we make friends and have good relationships with family and friends. Other episodes such as "Jealous Much" and "Don't React, Respond" focus on emotions that may come into play as children enter school and attempt to make and keep friends.

**Text Set 2: Making Friends and Bridging Differences**

This text set includes books that explore friendship, bullying, conflict, and resolution. Some of the characters are initially resistant to speak up for another person. After observing someone else's pain, some of the books show empathetic characters who exhibit concern and courage to make a difference. As a set, the books explore the importance of using stories to start conversations about compassion and empathy. Moreover, the overarching themes of empathy, kindness, and compassion are essential to the development of social-emotional learning in students.

deKinder, J. (2013). *Red*. Trans. by L. Watkinson. Grand Rapids, MI: Eerdmans Books for Young Readers.

Have you ever been embarrassed? Do you ever blush? Imagine if you were relentlessly teased because your cheeks turned red. In this powerful picture book, readers meet Tommy, a boy whose cheeks sometimes go from "tomato to strawberry to cherry red." When one of his friends gossips to classmates about Tommy's appearance, he asks them to stop. The group, including the class bully, laughs and teases Tommy until he is silenced and alone. Tommy's friend realizes that the joke has gone too far, and she must decide whether or not to stand up to the others or to remain quiet. After much self-reflection, the girl decides to speak up on Tommy's behalf. Her courage to defend her friend soon spreads to other students in the class. The power of this story is further accentuated by the red-and-black-hued illustrations.

Kerascoët. (2018). *I Walk with Vanessa: A Story about a Simple Act of Kindness*. New York, NY: Schwartz & Wade Books.

In this wordless picture book, Vanessa is bullied on her way home from school. Clearly, she is impacted and runs back to her house in tears. Another girl from Vanessa's neighborhood witnesses the event, and in a series of illustrated scenes, the artist clearly shows how much it has upset her. Throughout the rest of the evening, the incident continues to weigh on the little girl's mind. As readers view the double-page spread, they will notice that the little girl and Vanessa are clearly despondent over the situation. The next morning, the little girl invites Vanessa to walk with her and the other neighborhood children to school. Soon, many children walk in alliance with Vanessa. The wordless picture-book format works beautifully for students to discuss Vanessa's feelings and the actions taken by the little girl.

Woodson, J. (2012). *Each Kindness*. Ill. by E. B. Lewis. New York: Nancy Paulsen Books.

When Maya enters her new classroom, her attempts at making new friends are met with some resistance by the class bully, Chloe. Maya persists and brings in a jump rope or jacks to play with the girls. Unfortunately, the small group of girls whispers behind Maya's back, and eventually, she plays alone. When Maya doesn't come back to school the next day, the classroom teacher demonstrates the ripple effect of kindness. *"This is what kindness does, Ms. Albert said. Each little thing we do goes out, like a ripple, into the world."* Chloe suddenly realizes the errors of her actions and learns a difficult lesson in missed opportunities. The "not so happy" ending allows readers to pause and consider the overarching themes of this outstanding picture book.

**Text Set 2: Multimodal Activities and Extensions**

The books in this text set provide natural opportunities to discuss issues of bullying, compassion, and kindness. While there are a plethora of activities and extensions to promote a culture of kindness in today's classroom, using children's literature can spark rich conversations to guide students in their personal and social lives. Teachers and students can co-lead morning meetings to discuss issues and pose solutions.

Teachers can model kindness by extending greetings to the school nurse, office staff, and other school personnel. Students can follow suit and also write thank-you notes and messages to show their gratitude. In many schools, teachers and students integrate "kindness week" activities from resources such as "Random Acts of Kindness" (www.randomactsofkindness.org) or the "Kindness Curriculum" sponsored by University of Wisconsin–Madison's Center for Healthy Minds (https://centerhealthyminds.org/join-the-movement/sign-up-to-receive-the-kindness-curriculum). Teachers are encouraged to infuse children's books and related engagements about kindness throughout the year and not only during "kindness week."

Using a guided inquiry approach, teachers and students can respond to the "Color Your World with Kindness" video (www.youtube.com/watch?v=rwelE8yyY0U) and create a digital or print anchor chart with shared responses and examples of kind deeds and actions to emulate during the year. The video can also be viewed before launching a month-long kindness campaign or before reading any of the selections mentioned throughout this chapter. Students can also respond to the books through writing, art, and drama. Students can create a Tagxedo (www.tagxedo.com) or Wordle (www.wordle.net) to create a digital representation of ways to be kind and to take action. After reading any of the literature selections, students can use the Tellagami app (https://tellagami.com) to respond to the story and record its significance. For example, students can share their ideas about why it's important to be kind. Tellagami also provides a platform to convert the ideas into a class video that can be shared on a class page. As a class, students can also launch and participate in a kindness initiative in their school or surrounding community.

## ADDITIONAL RECOMMENDED BOOKS ABOUT SCHOOL

Arwen, H. (2019). *Have You Seen Mr. Robinson?* Adelaide, Australia: Starfish Bay Publishing.
Bailey, J. (2019). *Friend for Henry*. Ill. by M. Song. San Francisco, CA: Chronicle.
Berube, K. (2018). *Mae's First Day of School*. New York, NY: Abrams Books for Young Readers.
Bodeen, S. (2002). *Elizabeti's School*. Ill. by C. Hale. New York, NY: Lee and Low.
Boelts, M. (2007). *Those Shoes*. Ill. by N. Jones. Somerville, MA: Candlewick Press.
Burns, P. (2018). *Hello School*. New York, NY: Nancy Paulsen Books.
Harris, R. (2003). *I Am Not Going to School Today*. New York, NY: Margaret McElderry Books.
Hart-Sussman, H. (2013). *Noni Is Nervous*. Toronto, Canada: Tundra Books-Random House of Canada.
Ludwig, T. (2013). *The Invisible Boy*. Ill. by P. Barton. New York, NY: Alfred A. Knopf.
Pak, S. (2003). *Sumi's First Day of School*. New York, NY: Viking.
Penfold, A. (2018). *All Are Welcome*. Ill. by S. Kaufman. New York, NY: Alfred A. Knopf.
Roberts, J. (2014). *The Smallest Girl in the Smallest Grade*. Ill. by C. Robinson. New York, NY: Penguin Random House.

## AUTHOR/ILLUSTRATOR SPOTLIGHT: INTERVIEW WITH DERRICK BARNES

Derrick Barnes writes picture books, middle-grade novels, and young adult novels. He is the author of the award-winning book *Crown: Ode to the Fresh Cut* (2017) which won both a Newbery and Caldecott honor. He was also awarded the 2018 Ezra Jack Keats Award as an outstanding new writer. Like *The King of Kindergarten* (2019), his books feature and affirm African Americans through stories of families, friendship, and school. The Ruby Booker books offer young readers a chapter book series that chronicles Ruby's adventure as the only girl in a family with three brothers. He also maintains a blog called Raising the Mighty, where he reflects not only on his writing but also his raising of sons and his life outside of work. His next book takes him in a different direction with a nonfiction title, *Who's Got Game: Baseball*, to be published by Workman. You can visit him at https://derrickdbarnes.com.

*1. Please share your thinking about the importance of multicultural literature in the early childhood classroom.*

Having your bookshelves serve as mirrors and windows for the babies is imperative. These books will be an introduction to the vast ethnicities and various groups of people that exist on this planet. Teaching them early on, exposing them to people that don't look like them is the start of birthing human beings with opened minds.

*2. Some multicultural books affirm and explore identity. Explain how you do this in your books.*

I take universal experiences such as children heading to school for the first time, or what it feels like, afterward, to get a nice haircut or to be perfectly groomed, and simply put a beautiful black face on the protagonist. There was a point in time where there were no black faces on main characters unless we were runaway or happy-go-lucky slaves, downtrodden in urban environments, or the retelling of civil rights tales. It's so important to show us just being human, sprinkled in with the cultural nuances that make us different, which is not a bad thing. If I can show a child how people who look different have so much in common, and at the same time, teach them to appreciate the differences that we have, I've done my job as a writer.

*3. What advice would you give early childhood teachers as they attempt to explore concepts of identity with young children through multicultural literature?*

I think that I would introduce them to where the particular cultures that the book, whether they be fiction or nonfiction, come from so that we could begin an open discussion or create assignments around those specific mores and characteristics that are similar and dissimilar to their own cultures/household. For example, if I were to introduce to them a wonderful picture book titled *My Papi Has a Motorcycle* (2019) by Isabel Quintero and illustrated by Zeke Peña, I would first talk about the setting of the story, which happens to be Corona, California, and delve more into the history of the town, Mexican immigration, and all of the things that make the story distinct yet relatable, like the loving relationship between the girl protagonist and her father (papi). Then I'd introduce similar-themed books featuring characters of different ethnicities for comparison and to provide context (www.coronaca.gov/government/departments-divisions/library-recreation-services/library/heritage-room/history-of-corona).

*4. What are your hopes and dreams for early childhood classrooms and libraries in the future?*

My hope, from the artist/author perspective, in order to help out the educators, is that we (myself, other authors, illustrators of color, publishing companies, and editors) continue to provide children with books that tell such a broad range of stories to represent children of all races. Every child deserves to go to a bookstore or a library and be able to see a protagonist that looks like them. Every year an infographic is released by the Cooperative Children's Book Center, School of Education, University of Wisconsin–Madison. This graph creatively displays the ethnicity of the protagonists in children's books, and what percentage of that ethnic group is represented in books. Sadly, white characters make up 50 percent or more each year. What's worse is there are usually more animal protagonists than the number of black, Asian, Latinx, and Native Americans combined. We must keep working to change that, and educators can collectively demand it from publishers.

*5. Some teachers are hesitant to talk about diversity with young children. What words of encouragement can you offer them?*

I would tell them to be the catalyst of forward thinking when it comes to tolerance, compassion, and equality in the minds and lives of their young students. When many of these children go home, they are never taught the things that will allow them to relate to, appreciate, and communicate with people who do not look like them. If given the proper skills and information, they will be preparing those babies to go out into the world with open minds and the realization that we all want the same things out of life: opportunity, respect, understanding, and love.

## REFERENCES

Aboud, F. E., Mendelson, M. J., & Purdy, K. T. (2003). Cross-race peer relations and friendship quality. *International Journal of Behavioral Development, 27*(2), 165–173.

Bagwell, C., & Schmidt, M. (2011). *Friendships in childhood and adolescence.* New York, NY: Guilford Press.

Bukowski, W. M., Newcomb, A. F., & Hartup, W. W. (1996). *The company they keep: Friendship in childhood and adolescence.* New York, NY: Cambridge University Press.

Carter, C., & Nutbrown, C. (2016). A pedagogy of friendship: Young children's friendships and how schools can support them. *International Journal of Early Years Education, 24*(4), 395–413.

Crystal, D. S., Killen, M., & Ruck, M. (2008). It is who you know that counts: Intergroup contact and judgments about race-based exclusion. *British Journal of Developmental Psychology, 26*(1), 51–70.

Dunn, J. (2004). *Children's friendships: The beginnings of intimacy.* Oxford, UK: Blackwell Publishing.

Fink, E., & Hughes, C. (2019). Children's friendships. *The Psychologist, 32,* 28–31.

Gaias, L. M., Gal, D. E., Abry, T., Taylor, M., & Granger, K. L. (2018). Diversity exposure in preschool: Longitudinal implications for cross-race friendships and racial bias. *Journal of Applied Developmental Psychology, 59,* 5–15.

Gifford-Smith, M., & Brownell, C. (2003). Childhood peer relationships: Social acceptance, friendships, and peer networks. *Journal of School Psychology, 41*(4), 235–284.

Goularte, R. (2000). Social reality in the classroom: An alternate strategy for developing class rules. NCTE Elementary *Cyberbrief* 1.9. Retrieved from https://web.archive.org/web/20031214234233/http:/www1.ncte.org/library/files/Files/Cy%09berbriefs/Social_Reality_Class_Rules.pdf

Gronlund, N. E. (1959). *Sociometry in the classroom.* New York, NY: Harper.

Hartup, W. W. (1996). The company they keep: Friendships and their developmental significance. *Child Development, 67*(1), 1–13.

Hawley, P. (2002). Social dominance and prosocial and coercive strategies of resource control in preschoolers. *International Journal of Behavioral Development, 26*(2), 167–176.

Howes, C. (1996). The earliest friendships. In W. Bukowski, A. Newcomb, & W. Hartup (Eds.), *The company they keep: Friendship in childhood and adolescence* (pp. 66–86). Cambridge, UK: Cambridge University Press.

Hymel, S., & Swearer, S. M. (2015). Four decades of research on school bullying: An introduction. *American Psychologist, 70*(4), 293–299.

Hymel, S., Woody, E., & Bowker, A. (1993). Aggressive versus withdrawn unpopular children: variations in peer and self-perceptions in multiple domains. *Child Development, 64*(3), 879–896.

King, M. (2017, December 14). Encouraging a sense of gratitude in students. [Blog post]. Retrieved from https://www.edutopia.org/article/encouraging-sense-gratitude-students

Moreno, J. L. (1934). *A new approach to the problem of human interrelations.* Washington, DC: Nervous and Mental Disease Publishing.

National Association for the Education of Young Children. (2018). NAEYC Early Learning Program Accreditation Standards. Retrieved from www.naeyc.org/accreditation/early-learning/standards

Newgent, R. A., Lee, S. M., & Daniel, A. F. (2007). Interracial best friendships: Relationship with 10th graders' academic achievement level. *Professional School Counseling, 11*(2), 98–104.

Parsons, T. (1996). *Societies: Evolutionary and comparative practices.* Englewood Cliffs, NJ: Prentice Hall.

Pettigrew, T. F. (2008). Intergroup contact theory. *Annual Review of Psychology, 49*(1), 65–85.

Robinson, K. H., & Jones-Diaz, C. (2005). *Diversity and difference in early childhood education: Issues for theory and practice.* Berkshire, England: McGraw-Hill Education.

Rubin, K., Fredstrom, B., & Bowker, J. (2008). Future directions in . . . Friendship in childhood and early adolescence. *Social Development, 17*(4), 1085–1096.

Rutland, A., Killen, M., & Abrams, D. (2010). A new social-cognitive developmental perspective on prejudice: The interplay between morality and group identity. *Perspectives on Psychological Science, 5*(3), 279–291.

Smith-Bonahue, T., Smith-Adcock, S., & Ehrentraut, J. (2015). Preschool through kindergarten: "I won't be your friend if you don't!" Preventing and responding to relational aggression in preschool classrooms. *YC Young Children, 70*(1), 76–83.

Watson, K. (2018). "We are all friends": Disrupting friendship play discourses in inclusive early childhood education. *Contemporary Issues in Early Childhood, 20*(3), 253–264.

Wohlwend, K. (2007). Friendship meeting or blocking circle? Identities in the laminated spaces of a playground conflict. *Contemporary Issues in Early Childhood, 8*(1), 73–88.

## Additional Children's Literature Cited

Aliki. (1998). *Marianthe's story: Painted words and spoken memories.* New York, NY: Greenwillow Books.

Cohen, M. (1967/2009). *Will I have a friend.* New York, NY: Macmillan.

Ferry. B. (2015). *Stick and stone.* Ill. by T. Lichtenheld. Boston, MA: Houghton Mifflin.

Henkes, K. (1991). *Chrysanthemum.* New York, NY: Greenwillow Books.

Henkes, K. (1993) *Owen.* New York, NY: Greenwillow Books.

Lester, H. (1999). *Hooway for Wodney Wat.* Ill. by L. Munsinger. Boston, MA: Houghton Mifflin.

Lionni, L. (1963). *Swimmy.* New York, NY: Knopf.

Penn, A. (1993). *Kissing hand.* Washington, DC: Child & Family Press.

Pfister, M. (1992). *The rainbow fish.* New York, NY: North-South Books.

Raschka, C. (1993). *Yo? Yes!* New York, NY: Scholastic.

Rath, T., & Reckmeyer, M. (2009). *How full is your bucket?* Ill. by M. Manning. New York, NY: Gallup Press.

Slate, J. (1996). *Miss Bindergarten gets ready for kindergarten.* New York, NY: Dutton.

Woodson, J. (2012). *Each kindness.* Ill. by E. B. Lewis. New York, NY: Nancy Paulsen Books.

*Chapter Four*

# Partnering Within the Community

*Nurturing a Sense of Belonging*

- How can teachers find books that help children celebrate their own neighborhoods and community connections despite the ways society might devalue those contexts? What books help children reflect their relationships with grandparents, neighbors, and other community members?
- What books can help teachers talk with young children about the positives and negatives they see in their own communities and in their city or region more broadly?
- How can teachers share information about different kinds of neighborhoods and community connections in ways that respect all stakeholders, foster activism, and make children feel more a part of the community?

Schools and families are components of the broader neighborhood or local community in which children live and learn. Early childhood educators are tasked with navigating family connections as well as community influences in their students' social worlds. Children learn about themselves and others through their families and friendships, but also through connections they make outside the home and school. Children may have close relationships with extended family, neighbors, and other community members. They may also have questions about some aspects of their neighborhood and how they can connect with people in the community who are different from them or are facing challenges. This chapter focuses on books that honestly portray a variety of communities so that children can reflect on their own surroundings and relationships with both an affirming and critical lens. Many of these books grapple with what it means to be a good neighbor and a responsible citizen. Diverse neighborhoods and relationships with "unlikely" friends are explored, providing teachers with the chance to challenge students to see themselves in context and to become compassionate caretakers of themselves and those around them.

The Cambridge Dictionary defines *community* as "all the people who live in a particular area, or a group of people who are considered as a unit because of their shared interests or background" ("Community," n.d.). Community can certainly be conceptualized as the people in a neighborhood or set geographical area. Young children might interact regularly with and be curious about a variety of professionals (such as teachers, librarians, and doctors) and neighbors in their community. Families might forge community as they gather at farmer's markets, story times, sporting events, community gardens, or churches. In urban areas children might get to know their mail carriers, shop owners, bus drivers, or community-based police officers. Friendships might form on the block or on the playground and may expand into family friendships with intergenerational connections as grandparents or elderly neighbors cross paths. All of these potential stakeholders in the community play a role in the lives of children.

According to a National Education Association (2008) policy brief, "It takes a village to raise a child is a popular proverb with a clear message: the whole community has an essential role to play in the growth and development of its young people" (unpaged). While this proverb may be appealing in its simplicity, the question of how teachers can engage the "village" in ways that foster good citizenship in both their students and the adults in their lives is far more complex. What would meaningful interconnections between school, home, and community look like? How can teachers use books to explore some of the more complicated or controversial dimensions of community?

Children grow emotionally, intellectually, and physically through both their personal relationships and their community. According to the Children's Bureau (n.d.), for young people, "a sense of community brings connection both to their surroundings and the individuals in those surroundings—further connecting them to their own unique place in the world" (unpaged). Community can be found at school, in the neighborhood, and through relationships with a range of individuals in a child's life.

When *Something Beautiful* (Wyeth) was published in 1998, educators and librarians were struck by the direct images and language related to an impoverished urban experience. This book has endured over time as a way to help children celebrate their own communities and find ways to be proud of their surroundings. Children from all socioeconomic backgrounds and geographic regions need to see themselves represented in books, and teachers need to feel empowered to have difficult conversations about topics such as food instability and housing insecurity, interactions with aging populations, and valuing all members of the local community. Learning about the community and community helpers is a typical part of the elementary school curriculum, but the books in this chapter invite teachers and children to consider relationships with vulnerable members of the community as well as leaders in the community. While it might be tempting to focus on idealized portrayals of community, "research shows that young children are emotionally and socially perceptive in ways that might easily be underestimated" (Thompson & Thompson, 2015, p. 33). Rather than underestimate children, early childhood educators can choose books that challenge their students to reflect on their community, build on the relationships they value, and possibly effect change in their communities.

Like *Something Beautiful,* books such as *Everybody Cooks Rice* (Dooley, 1991) and *Madlenka* (Sis, 2000) capture the importance of getting to know your community. *Madlenka* functions much like a geography book, while *Everybody Cooks Rice* (and similar titles by the same author) celebrates commonalities across cultures. Both books invite teachers and children to compare their own communities to those in the books, asking questions about the people around them who are similar and different in various ways. At the heart of community is the relationships children form with people and places. According to the National Council for the Social Studies (NCSS, 2010), early childhood educators can rely on lessons in "human geography" to help prepare children to become informed and active citizens in their local community. Books and curricular activities that help children develop a sense of place are important because they focus on both "the physical world around them and the social and cultural world they share with others" (Brillante & Mankiw, 2015, p. 17). Classroom projects that investigate physical environments and geography have curricular and cognitive benefits as well as the potential to foster social and emotional growth. In fact, developing a sense of place is linked to a sense of belonging. Epstein's (2009) research demonstrates that a sense of belonging contributes to children's overall social and emotional development and is an essential aspect of school readiness.

As with friendships and family, it is important that teachers invite children to reflect on their unique community and learn about it alongside peers. Noddings (2005) recommends that "perhaps the most important thing we educators can do as we pursue community is to study it and to share what is learned with our students. . . . Students need not only to belong to a community; even more, they need to know what it means and can mean to belong to a community. Education for community life requires both self-knowledge and collective-knowledge" (p. 267). These books reflect both kinds of knowledge, some focused on the familiar and others on community awareness.

This collective knowledge leads to a question of citizenship and ways to foster the notion of "caring communities" through classroom instruction. According to Lemieux and Neal (2010), "caring communities" focus on good citizenship, empathy, and connecting essential values to daily interactions. Similarly, the National Council for the Social Studies (2013) describes the importance of "civic virtues," which include traits that enable children to become citizens who contribute to the common good through civic engagement. In addition, the early childhood standards include goals such as "explain how all people, not just official leaders, play important roles in a community" (D2.Civ.2.K-2). Two important aspects of community to explore with young children using picture books include how people experiencing homelessness and the elderly are included and valued.

Based on census information and United Nations reports, young children are increasingly likely to have exposure to and relationships with older people (Robinson & Howatson-Jones, 2014). In fact, "it is a rare child who does not have the opportunity to interact with older adults in the form of relatives or community members, and grandparents often play a particularly significant role in children's lives" (Crawford & Bhattacharya, 2014, p. 129). Even though there is clear evidence that children are living in households with grandparents and extended family members, portrayals of those kind of families are lacking in children's books. The literature that does feature children interacting with grandparents and older adults often tells stories of celebrations and traditions. This focus is appropriate, especially as it relates to the work teachers might do to help children feel more connected as part of an intergenerational community. Children's books have the potential to reflect the kind of relationships children have with older adults and to nurture attitudes about older people more broadly. Robinson and Howatson-Jones (2014) studied children's views of older people and found that they held stereotypes rather than being ageist. Their key findings indicate that "the more familiar they are, generally, the more positive is their attitude" (p. 306), thus suggesting that exposure to positive portrayals can make a difference in building knowledge, empathy, and skills related to older people. Children need affirmation of their relationships with older people and also information about the kinds of challenges these elders face. Books such as *Wilfred Gordon McDonald Partridge* (Fox, 1989) and *Nana Upstairs and Nana Downstairs* (dePaola, 1998) have endured as books that portray compassionate children interacting with loved ones who are struggling with age-related issues. Teachers are drawn to these books because of the positive role models, but there is also a need to infuse diverse titles to ensure that all children see themselves and members of their communities in stories.

Just as older populations are growing in the United States and across the globe, "homeless families with very young children are one of the fastest growing segments of homelessness" (Swick, 2004, p. 299). Families experiencing homeless or food instability are part of our classrooms and rely on the community for support. How can young children navigate friendships with peers who are experiencing these challenges? In what ways can teachers help children living in these situations feel valued and included? Author Eve Bunting has attempted to tackle this topic in books such as *Fly Away Home* (1991) and *December* (1997), but more titles with diverse characters that capture the complexity of experiences of people struggling with housing need to be shared in the classroom. For the purposes of this chapter, the selections include titles that can reduce both the invisibility and the shame associated with families facing homelessness or food insecurity.

As teachers select stories to share with their students, they will want to keep in mind to include selections that move beyond traditional tropes and themes. Considering stories that will help students read the realities of their world will afford them with opportunities to discuss how authors portray these struggles humanely and with a critical lens. While stories will not "celebrate" these experiences, teachers can select books that feature compelling stories and art alongside relatable and realistic characters. A classic title that meets this criterion is the Caldecott Honor Book titled *A Chair for My Mother* (Williams, 1982). In this story, the family saves money to restore their lives following a fire that burned all of their possessions in their home. The generosity demonstrated by their neighbors and extended family shows readers the strength of community as the family is now able to afford a big comfy chair for their new home. Realistic fiction stories like this will expand students' thinking about poverty beyond the images they may see in the media or in folklore.

Children are widely exposed to folktales that include poverty as part of the narrative, such as "The Matchstick Girl," "Stone Soup," and "Jack and the Beanstalk." These books were not included as part of the recommended texts, nor were historical fiction books about topics such as the Great Depression or Reconstruction that address poverty directly. Instead, the recommended community-based text sets include recently published, realistic fiction books with diverse families and straightforward themes related to poverty and homelessness. The elementary students in the classroom encounter described below consider the impact of coming together as a community to enrich the lives of others.

## CLASSROOM VIGNETTE: *YOU AND ME AND HOME SWEET HOME*

After the first and second graders in Mrs. H.'s multiage class read *You and Me and Home Sweet Home* (2009) by George Ella Lyon and illustrated by Stephanie Anderson, many of her students made an immediate connection to the realities of poverty in today's society. The students recognized that many people in their surrounding community live in poverty and do not have a space to call their own. During the class discussion, the students talked about

Habitat for Humanity (www.habitat.org) and the concept of building houses for people in need. Mrs. H.'s students posed a myriad of questions related to the logistics of this endeavor, as demonstrated in the following exchange.

Student 1: How do they get the brick?

Student 2: They, like, donate stuff. It's charity.

Student 1: And doors? And dishwashers?

Student 2: Yeah, even that!

Student 1: What about clothes?

Mrs. H.: There are places like churches and Community Aid where people can go to get clothes for free or for a discount.

Student 3: Oh yeah, Community Aid! My aunt goes there! And food kitchens, like in *Last Stop on Market Street*!

Mrs. H.: That's right! Great text-to-text connection! There are places like in *Last Stop on Market Street* (de la Peña, 2015) that are often called soup kitchens where people can go and eat a meal if they do not have food of their own.

Student 4: You know there's stuff that you can donate at the school or at grocery stores, like boxes? I was going to do one, I had all of these toys in the box, but I could never do it alone.

Me: It was great that you had the desire to help someone like that! There are a lot of ways to help people all around us. Maybe we can take some time to think of ways that we can help people, and then plan to follow through with our ideas.

Student 3: Say that people don't have anything. They must sleep outside. If, say, I were a daddy, I would move, and then I would go to them and say, "We moved so you could get a house, and here's some money so you could get some stuff."

Student 5: That's so nice of you! Then they could have both!

Mrs. H. further explained that one of her students saw construction workers at a local amusement park and connected the story to all the hard work that the workers did to make a new roller coaster. The student observed that it took many members of Mama's and Sharonda's community to build their new house. This connection resonated powerfully for some of his friends who also loved roller coasters and had never thought about all the work that went into making them. They realized that it is a lot of work to make a house, too. Mrs. H.'s class talked about how a roller coaster must be built so it is strong and safe to ride on, and how a house, too, must be built in a way that keeps the weather out and is safe and strong for people to live in. As Mrs. H.'s class read the book, they imagined being in Sharonda's shoes and what it would be like to see a new house being built right before "their" eyes. One student was in the process of moving into a new house, and he shared his feelings about watching the construction and explained that he could connect with the main character's feelings of happiness. A lot of students became worried about the safety of people building Sharonda's home, and the class researched and learned about building safety. The students also were impressed with how quickly Sharonda's house was built with so much help.

Mrs. H.'s class talked about what the last night would be like before moving into a new house. They shared that they would feel nervous, anxious, and excited. Several students commented that they wouldn't be able to sleep and shared their final reflections:

Student 7: Sharonda was probably feeling happy at the end! They made the world a better place for her!

Student 3: Yeah, like I could take a water vacuum and clean up all of that junk in the ocean!

Mrs. H: What an awesome idea! What else can we do to make the world a better place?

Student 8: I would like to help people with peace, teach people about peace. I would tell them that peace is good. I could read a book about peace to people.

Student 4: My Bubby cleans the floor with the vacuum, and sometimes I help!

Student 2: I can become a police officer and help keep the community be safe.

Student 1: Remember that big pile of trash in the ocean that we learned about? I want to clean that up. I also want to clean up the trash on the land. I will pick it up, walk around the world, and pick up a lot of stuff.

Student 5: I want to plant trees! If there is a tree in need, I would help it out. I will water the trees, so we all have oxygen.

Student 6: I will plant flowers! Then the world would look pretty.

Student 10: I can help other people clean up their yard and get their trucks out of the snow when they're stuck!

The students were very excited to come up with their own ideas to help others, and conversations about the book continued throughout the ensuing days.

Mrs. H. also shared how she extended the book with her students:

> We took the time to place ourselves in the shoes of others who have less than we do. We mapped out a small space within the classroom as the home for our whole family and listed what we had and what we did not have, if we were like Sharonda and Mama at the beginning of the book. We imagined what life would be like from day to day and how that is different from what we are used to. We talked about how powerful it is when a group of people come together and donate their time and efforts to do something kind. To put this idea in action, we took a field trip to a local nature area and worked together on a service-learning project for the camp. The students cleaned up hiking paths for visitors and restocked the community wood pile for campfires.
>
> My husband came in and we shared with the kids how a group of our friends is helping to build a café in a town with many people who are of low income. The café will be a place of positivity and aid for those who are in need. We talked about the different tools needed in construction, such as hammers, nails, measuring tapes, and saws. We shared pictures with the class, and they began to imagine how they could help in a similar situation. They gave us ideas on what the café could look like and shared helpful things that the people running the café could do to help their local community. This especially hit home for one student whose mom started her own café near his home. He excitedly shared that process and the important lessons that his mom learned along the way.
>
> We talked about different ways that we can be "world changers" and what we can collectively do to make the world a better place. With my help, the students typed up their ideas and we turned them into an oration project. Individually, students practiced speaking skills as they shared what they wrote. Finally, they presented their final orations to the rest of the class as well as to another class that we invited to come listen.

## MULTIMODAL TEXT SETS

### Text Set 1: Making Intergenerational Connections

The books in this set feature young children, grandparents, and elderly neighbors. Grandparents provide a sense of trust and a way to pass along cultural and family traditions. The selections showcase powerful intergenerational interactions co-constructed by children and elders in their families and community.

Castillo, L. (2014). *Nana in the City*. Boston, MA: Clarion/Houghton Mifflin Harcourt.

This Caldecott Medal–winning book features a child visiting his grandmother who lives in an apartment in the city. The boy is excited to see his Nana but does not think the city is a good place to live. He thinks it's loud and scary. Can his Nana convince him that it is bustling and booming not loud, that it is extraordinary rather than scary? She attempts to show him the joy of city living by exploring together and interacting with street performers, dog walkers, and homeless people. This beautifully illustrated book shows the bond that is built between a grandparent and grandchild when they spend quality time together and truly get to know each other.

Le, M. (2018). *Drawn Together*. Ill. by D. Santat. New York, NY: Hyperion.

In this beautifully illustrated and compelling picture book, a young boy has a difficult time communicating with his Thai-speaking grandfather. After a series of attempts to communicate and find similar interests, the young boy retreats to another room to draw illustrations. Then, to his surprise, his grandfather shares the illustrations in his own sketchbook. Together, they discover that they are "drawn together" through their love of art. By sharing their creativity, this intergenerational pair find a common interest and build on their love of stories.

Love, J. (2018). *Julián Is a Mermaid*. Somerville, MA: Candlewick Press.

In this award-winning picture book, readers meet a young boy, Julián, and his *abuela* as they board the subway along with three beautiful mermaids. Enamored by their beautiful gowns with flowing hair and tails, Julián imagines himself as a mermaid. In a series of wordless pages, readers sense Julián's deep love and affection for mermaids. His dream-like sequence of sinking deep into the ocean to swim alongside the sea creatures results in being gifted with a beautiful tail. At home, Julián announces, "Abuela, I am also a mermaid" and customizes an original mermaid outfit. His grandmother provides him with one last accessory before they walk to New York's Annual Mermaid Parade. Throughout the story, Julián's grandmother encourages his imagination and supports his creative play.

Smalls, I. (2006). *My Pop Pop and Me*. New York, NY: Little, Brown & Company.

In this beautifully illustrated story in rhyme, a little boy and his grandfather enjoy the afternoon baking a delicious lemon bar cake. The first page shows the special bond between a grandfather and his grandson as they begin their baking adventure, from scrubbing their hands to pouring the batter. The simple rhyme schemes ("Pour pour that's what batter's for") along with action verbs ("creak, creak, "slurp, slurp," and "slosh, slosh") signal the progress of their collaborative baking project. As they follow the steps to make a yummy cake, the illustrations signal affection, joy, and delight. At the end of the book, there is a step-by-step guide for readers to make their own lemon bar cake.

**Text Set 1: Multimodal Activities and Extensions**

The books in this set feature children learning about the relationships they can have with older members of their community, including their grandparents. The selections contribute to developing positive relationships and social-emotional well-being of young children and the elderly while supporting the curriculum. Teachers can use the books as an opportunity to build intergenerational connections and outreach opportunities. Infusing opportunities for young children to interact with their elders will provide them with positive perceptions while listening to stories, sharing activities, and finding commonalities.

Teachers can promote multigenerational activities within their curriculum by inviting grandparents to their classroom to share their hobbies and stories. They may share a special talent like playing an instrument or a favorite recipe. Teachers can also forge a relationship with a retirement home community or start a service-learning project. Teachers may want to check with the Institute on Aging (www.nia.nih.gov) and Generations United National Database to find established intergenerational programs (www.gu.org/ig-program-database/page/60).

Students can express appreciation to their grandparents and older people in their lives by sending them homemade greeting cards, writing letters, or creating a recorded greeting using Vacaroo (https://vocaroo.com), Voki (www.voki.com) or ChatterPix Kids (https://apps.apple.com/us/app/chatterpix-kids/id734046126).

After reading *Drawn Together*, students and elderly friends can illustrate a picture together or engage in other art activities to foster communication. Students can also help elderly members develop and design a memory book with photographs, artifacts, and digital media to share family stories. Students can use SmileBox (www.smilebox.com) or Storybird (https://storybird.com) to create memory books or to compose stories. Using the StoryCorps App (https://storycorps.org/participate/storycorps-app), students can interview their elders to celebrate their lives. Teachers can refer to Story-

Corps Education for additional resources and lesson plans to support oral storytelling and community-building initiatives (https://storycorps.org/discover/education). Students can also read stories, perform songs or plays (e.g., using Sock Puppets, https://apps.apple.com/us/app/sock-puppets-complete/id547666894), or help members of their community with gardening. There are countless ways for teachers to embark on intergenerational learning programs within their curriculum. The following resources include several pathways to support these engagements:

- https://legacyproject.org/activities/activitiesag.html
- https://storycorps.org/participate/storycorps-app

## Text Set 2: Understanding Housing Challenges and Socioeconomic Diversity

The books in this text set illuminate issues of poverty, income disparities, and food insecurity. Conversations and stories about real-world issues help to prepare students to cope with or consider social problems and economic injustices. The books also serve as a springboard to invite students to problem-solve and become caring, informed, and proactive citizens.

Boelts, M. (2007). *Those Shoes*. Somerville, MA: Candlewick Press.

Jeremy dreams of wearing the latest black high-tops with two white stripes, but his Grandma points out, "There's no room for 'want' around here—just 'need.'" The next day at recess, Jeremy's shoes break, so he visits the guidance counselor to borrow some shoes. The only pair that fit Jeremy were childish with yellow ducks and Velcro. When Jeremy returns to his classroom, all of his friends, except for Antonio, laugh at him. Sensing the urgency, Grandma takes Jeremy to find a pair of shoes. They visit several thrift shops until Jeremy spots "those shoes." Even though the shoes are too small, Jeremy uses his own money to purchase them. The next day, Jeremy notices that his friend Antonio's shoes are held together with tape and that his feet are a bit smaller. Despite Jeremy's fondness for "those shoes," he decides to give them to his friend Antonio. This realistic picture book with themes of financial insecurity, bullying, and kindness will spark important conversations with readers.

de la Peña, M. (2015). *Last Stop on Market Street*. Ill. by C. Robinson. New York, NY: Putnam.

This picture book takes the reader on a bus ride through a neighborhood that includes "broken streetlamps" and "boarded-up stores." CJ and his nana observe and interact with their fellow riders along the way, including "the

Sunglass Man," a guitar player, a blind man, and an "old woman with curlers and butterflies in a jar." De la Pena's evocative descriptions and Robinson's collage art pair perfectly to convey the beauty of the community of people on the bus and in the neighborhood. The book pays respect to everyone and everything CJ and Nana encounter, most importantly the familiar faces at the soup kitchen where they exit the bus. As the two serve a meal to those in need in their community, it is clear to readers that beauty can be found anywhere if you open your eyes and your heart.

Durango, J. (2017). *The One Day House.* Watertown, MA: Charlesbridge Publishing.

A young boy named Wilson has lots of ideas for improvements to his Gigi's house. He wants to fix the windows, stairs, and chimney. He shares his ideas with friends and neighbors, including his teacher and librarian. Could a community organization called "Build Up Neighbors" help Wilson help his grandmother? As the book progresses, each page features one of the potential improvements to Gigi's home with Wilson's vision for the repair on one side and the current state of the house on the other. This book captures Wilson's love of his neighborhood and Gigi's home and shows how a community can come together to improve housing.

Lyon, G. E. (2009). *You and Me and Home Sweet Home.* Ill by. S. Anderson. New York, NY: Atheneum Books for Young Readers.

Author George Ella Lyon's personal experience and participation in a Women's Build Project in Kentucky inspired her to write about the realities that many people face. At the beginning of the story, Sharonda and her mother have been temporarily living at her aunt's apartment. When their local church decides to build them a house, Sharonda observes the dedication of the volunteers and the building process. She could "drive the first nail" into the sturdy wood and also helps with the window boxes that will "bloom with flowers" in the spring. The beautiful watercolor and pastel pencil illustrations enhance the story's theme of hope, partnering with the community, and taking action.

**Text Set 2: Multimodal Activities and Extensions**

The books in this set all feature selections that will allow students to discuss and broaden their perspectives about real-world social and economic issues. The realistic stories showcase themes of resilience, community partnerships, housing insecurities, financial distress, and social action. Teachers can use these books as an opportunity to integrate service-learning projects while designing inquiry-based learning experiences to support all areas of the curriculum.

For example, after reading *Those Shoes* (Boelts, 2009), students can use digital or print images from magazines to sort "needs and wants" as a class. Teachers can encourage home-school connections by inviting parents/guardians to extend the question of "What makes a need or a want?"

Teachers can also invite students to discuss the concept of "volunteering" and "giving back to others." After generating a list of possibilities, teachers and students can participate in a service-learning project, such as coordinating a food, clothing, toy, book, or personal care items drive with a local agency. Some additional suggestions can be found at the Kid World Citizen blog (https://kidworldcitizen.org/35-service-projects-for-kids). It is important for teachers to keep in mind that service-learning projects should include multiple opportunities for students to question why the need for the service even exists. As teachers and students co-construct new understandings about the books in this text set, it's critical that they explore how they can become involved to make a difference in their communities.

After reading *The One Day House* (Durango, 2017) and *You and Me and Home Sweet Home* (Lyon, 2009), teachers can launch conversations about how students can help others in their neighborhood. Inviting guest speakers from the local community to discuss housing insecurity and to share resources will also guide whole-class discussions. Teachers of young children can also incorporate resources available through "Sesame Street in Communities" (https://sesamestreetincommunities.org/topics/family-homelessness) to support conversations with their class. For slightly older students, teachers can infuse resources from the National Alliance to End Homelessness (https://endhomelessness.org) and visit the following sites for additional suggestions:

- Parents and Kids Talk about Homelessness: www.youtube.com/watch?v=CX4TzWdDAFY
- Homeless Global Learning Project: http://homelessglp.weebly.com/lesson-activities.html

Students can learn more about how kids can help Habitat for Humanity from www.habitat.org/stories/how-can-kids-help-habitat. Students can also write collaborative or individual letters to their local and state representatives advocating for additional resources and awareness for homeless children and families. It is important for teachers to keep in mind that service-learning projects should include multiple opportunities for students to question why the service is needed.

## Text Set 3: Neighborhood Appreciation and Transformation

The books in this set feature young children and their families exploring and enjoying their neighborhoods. The neighborhoods featured are diverse, inviting, and vibrant. Individuals are celebrated for their unique contributions to the community, and the neighborhoods are highlighted for specific attributes and overall strengths. Readers will find themselves drawn to these neighborhoods and the people in them.

Archer, M. (2019). *Daniel's Good Day*. New York, NY: Nancy Paulsen Books.

What does a good day in the city look like for a bus driver, crossing guard, or mail carrier? This book takes a young child of color on an exploration to find out. As Daniel walks to his grandmother's house, he interacts with his neighbors and friends, asking, "What makes a good day for you?" The replies vary, each one making Daniel even more curious about his neighbors and creating a sense of community. The collage effects and rich, saturated colors make the book child-centered and joyful. Daniel's independence, his interest in getting to know his neighbors, and his familial relationships make this a great fit for early childhood classrooms.

Casal, M. (2019). *My Town's (Extra) Ordinary People*. Munich, Germany: Prestel Publishing.

Theo, the young narrator of this book, introduces readers to twenty-two of his neighbors. As Theo explains, each of these neighbors has "something that makes them unique, special, and interesting." The book functions almost like a portrait gallery, as each neighbor is featured on their own page with accompanying art and text. The descriptions are full of detail and charm, and Theo tells stories about each of the featured people. Carla spends her time in the park bringing seeds for the birds, Glenn plays piano every day at 6:45 p.m., and Ogden is a waiter by day but as astronomer in his apartment by night. The illustrations feature muted colors and matte finish, which fits with the funky and eccentric feel of the book.

Liu, J. (2019). *My City*. Munich, Germany: Prestel Publishing.

Small print on the first page of this book reads "Max can bring a letter to the mailbox all by himself today." Max departs his home with letter in hand and sets off for a full day's adventure. He passes cyclists, buses, and trash trucks. He walks by a laundromat, grocery store, and museum. The story unfolds on full-bleed, double-page spreads with shifting perspectives. On one page, Max is dwarfed by marathoners; in another his face looms large as he stares into the night sky. *My City* functions as a nearly wordless book and might be mistaken as simple, but details such as the blue crayon scribbles on the endpapers, Max's cat, signs for a lost dog, and the path of a particular yellow leaf add layers of sophistication and mystery to the story.

Quintero, I. (2019). *My Papi Has a Motorcycle*. Ill. by Z. Pena. New York, NY: Kokila.

A librarian, a postal worker, construction workers, small business owners, grandparents, and even stray cats are included as part of the community in this book. Daisy, clad in a purple helmet and blue glasses, hops on her dad's motorcycle when he gets home from his job as a carpenter. They zigzag and zoom through the streets of their neighborhood, making the usual stops and seeking new adventures. They are disappointed when they find their favorite *raspados* (shaved ice) shop is out of business. The illustrations were created digitally, and the colors are muted but cheery. The action is conveyed through varied page layouts and changes in perspective; the pair often ride off the page. In addition, the inclusion of some panel art and speech bubbles helps maintain the story's lively pace and joyful theme. Daisy loves her neighborhood and can reflect on its past and future because of her relationship with her dad and others in her community.

**Text Set 3: Multimodal Activities and Extensions**

The books in this set all feature children learning about their neighborhoods and getting to know people in their community. Teachers can use these books as an opportunity to bring guest speakers into the classroom, enhance geography skills, and improve descriptive writing. In addition, all of these titles celebrate community by focusing on what makes a community unique. Teachers can foster children's knowledge of and connection to their own neighborhoods through the activities and extensions related to this book.

After meeting the characters in *My Town's (Extra) Ordinary People*, students can brainstorm a list of people in their community they believe are extraordinary. The list might include barbers, police officers, librarians, bus drivers, and small business owners. These individuals can be invited to the classroom for children to meet and learn more about. Students can develop specific questions to ask the guests in advance. A KWL (Know/Want to Know/Learned) chart could be useful in helping children with this. They can also create art as a gift for the speaker. A digital option for this could be offered by utilizing a tools such as reallycolor.com or pixlr.com, which turn photographs into coloring pages or allow for other creative alterations.

Taking a neighborhood walk will help young children see their surroundings with new eyes. Teachers can start by helping children make observations about their classroom and even mapping their schools. PBS provides a child-friendly tool for this (www.pbs.org/parents/crafts-and-experiments/

you-can-map-this-and-that). To expand beyond the classroom, students can learn to locate their school and home on a map. This can be done both on a paper map and using tools such as Google Maps, and students can then render their own versions (perhaps like the one featured on the endpapers of *My Papi Has a Motorcycle*). National Geographic offers additional resources for helping children with map skills (www.nationalgeographic.org/news/map-it-young-children). Another way to have students think about the geography of their home area is to compare pictures from the past with the way the area currently looks. The photographs might make the maps more understandable and enable them to ask further questions about their neighborhood.

The Fred Rogers Center (www.fredrogerscenter.org) offers a range of resources for early childhood teachers as they try to harness the "power of human connection" through their classroom interactions. The center partners with the University of Pittsburgh and the Harvard Graduate School of Education to offer Simple Interactions (www.simpleinteractions.org). This program and the Everyday Interactions site (www.everydayinteractions.org/videos-featured) embrace the philosophy of Fred Rogers and his commitment to knowing your community. Everyday Interactions features videos such a "Walk around the Block," while others address daily routines and how to be a part of a group.

## ADDITIONAL RECOMMENDED BOOKS ABOUT COMMUNITY

Ada, A. F. (2002). *I Love Saturdays y Domingos*. Ill. by E. Savadier. New York, NY: Atheneum Books for Young Readers.

Ancona, G. (2015). *Can We Help? Kids Volunteering in the Community*. New York, NY: Philomel.

Becker, K. M. (2013). *My Dream Playground*. Ill. by J. Henry. Somerville, MA: Candlewick Press.

Brandt, L. (2014). *Maddi's Fridge*. Ill. by V. Vogel. Brooklyn, NY: Flashlight Press.

Brown, T. F. (2010). *Around our Way on Neighbors' Day*. Ill. by C. Riley-Webb. New York, NY: Abrams Books for Young Readers.

Bunting, E. (2015). *Yard Sale*. Ill. by L. Castillo. Somerville, MA: Candlewick Press.

Campbell, M., & Luyken, C. (2018). *Adrian Simcox Does NOT Have a Horse*. New York, NY: Dial Books for Young Readers.

Campoy, I. (2016). *Maybe Something Beautiful*. Boston, MA: Houghton Mifflin Harcourt.

Coehlo, J., & Colpoys, A. (2019). *Grandpa's Stories*. New York, NY: Abrams Books for Young Readers.

Collier, B. (2004). *Uptown*. New York, NY: Henry Holt.

Cumpiano, I. (2005). *Quinito's Neighborhood*. Ill. by J. Ramirez. San Franciso, CA: Children's Book Press.

DiSalvo, D. (2001). *A Castle on Viola Street*. New York, NY: HarperCollins Publishers.

Ellis, E. (2019). *The Truth about Grandparents*. New York, NY: Little, Brown & Company.

Essa, H. (2019). *Common Threads: Adam's Day at the Market*. Ill. by M. Tous. Ann Arbor, MI: Sleeping Bear Press.

Flett, J. (2019). *Birdsong*. Berkeley, CA: Greystone Books.

Guidroz, R. (2019). *Leila in Saffron*. Ill. by D. Mirtalipova. New York, NY: Salaam Reads.

Gunning, M. (2004). *A Shelter in Our Car*. Ill. by E. Pedlar. New York, NY: Lee & Low Books.

Horrocks, A. (2010). *Silas' Seven Grandparents*. Ill. by H. Flook. Victoria, BC: Orca Publishers.
Hudes, Q. A. (2010). *Welcome to My Neighborhood*. Ill. by S. Arihara. New York, NY: Scholastic.
Isadora, R. (2010). *Say Hello*. New York, NY: G.P. Putnam and Sons.
Liu, S. (2016). *A Morning with Grandpa*. Ill. by C. Forshay. New York, NY: Lee & Low Books.
Meddour, W. (2019). *Grandpa's Top Threes*. Ill. by D. Egneus. Somerville, MA: Candlewick Press.
Melmed, L. K. (2018). *Daddy, Me and the Magic Hour*. Ill. by S. Rich. New York, NY: Sky Pony Press.
Oh, J. (2019). *Our Favorite Day*. Somerville, MA: Candlewick Press.
Raschka, C. (2005). *The Hello, Goodbye Window*. New York, NY: Hyperion Books.
Rockliff, M. (2009). *The Busiest Street in Town*. Ill. by S. McMenemy. New York, NY: Alfred A. Knopf.
Smith, H. (2019). *A Plan for Pops*. Ill. by B. Kerrigan. Victoria, BC: Orca Books.
Verde, S. (2018). *Hey, Wall*. Ill. by J. Parra. New York, NY: Simon & Schuster Books for Young Readers.

## AUTHOR/ILLUSTRATOR SPOTLIGHT: INTERVIEW WITH MATT DE LA PEÑA

Award-winning author Matt de la Peña has published seven young adult novels (including *Mexican WhiteBoy, We Were Here,* and *Superman: Dawnbreaker*) and five picture books (including *Love* and *Last Stop on Market Street*). In 2016, he was recognized for standing up for intellectual freedom by the National Council of Teachers of English and received the NCTE Intellectual Freedom Award. Matt earned his MFA in creative writing from San Diego State University and his BA from the University of the Pacific (UOP), where he attended school on a full athletic basketball scholarship. In 2019, he received an honorary doctorate from UOP. Matt has inspired countless readers and teachers throughout the country. He shares his passion for storytelling by teaching creative writing, presenting at national conferences, and visiting schools and universities. Matt has received national recognition and accolades for his body of work, including the Pura Belpré Honor for *The Living* (2014) and the Newbery Medal for *Last Stop on Market Street* (illustrated by Christian Robinson). Matt's website—http://mattdelapena.com—includes a wealth of information, including numerous press interviews.

*1. Please share your thinking about the importance of multicultural literature in the early childhood classroom.*

It's important to have diverse literature in classrooms full of diverse kids, obviously. It's empowering to see yourself reflected in books. But it's just as important to bring diverse literature into more homogenous classrooms. For some kids it may be their only opportunity to see the world through the eyes of another. And when you try on the perspective of "others" at a young age, you are more likely to move through the world with empathy. It's great to have books with diverse perspectives at home, but it's just as important to have them at school.

*2. Some multicultural books affirm and explore identity. Explain how you do this in your books.*

My approach has evolved over the years. I used to exclusively write books that explored race and class head on. But now I also write books that feature diverse characters in storylines that aren't (at least overtly) about race or class. Race and class exploration in these books is more subtle. It's the layer beneath the more visible storyline. My main objective these days is to write books that are inclusive.

*3. Select one of your favorite books or poems, and share how you would explore it with young learners.*

I like introducing young readers to the book *Each Kindness* by Jaqueline Woodson. First, we read the story and I let them guide the discussion that comes after. If they are simply focused on the surface of the story, we stay with that for a while. Usually, though, they find the deeper levels of the story on their own. If not, I ask questions. I've never had an experience with that book where young people don't eventually get to the deeper story. But each experience with a book and a group of kids is unique and should be treated as such. One of the coolest aspects of literature is how the story can be many different things depending on who's reading it and when the reading is taking place. So much of the literary experience is the context in which the story is experienced.

*4. What advice would you give early childhood teachers as they attempt to explore concepts of identity with young children through multicultural literature?*

I think it's vital to remain humble. We often think as educators we are supposed to have the answers. And we feel embarrassed when we don't, when we're introducing a story on which we are not an expert. But I would argue this is the best place to be as a teacher. Students should see us grappling with meaning, too. Trying to understand themes. Going down dead-end roads and starting over. Great literature isn't about right answers. It's about generating interesting questions.

*5. What classroom suggestions can you provide for teachers to select and incorporate diverse books into their curriculum?*

I think it's great when teachers follow online discussions about what books are culturally accurate and respectful. We Need Diverse Books does a great job offering tools for teacher. And I'm learning so much from the online discussions tagged #DisruptTexts. And one of the most powerful gestures an educator can make is having a classroom library that is equitable.

*6. What are your hopes and dreams for early childhood classrooms and libraries in the future?*

I'm starting to see it on the road. Teachers everywhere are going the extra mile to find culturally relevant books to share with their students. We know how important great teachers are in the lives of young people. How about a great teacher who is intentional about the stories he or she brings into the classroom? My dream is that we will one day have leadership who invests much more into education. I have young children myself. I wish their teachers made a lot more money. Because there's not a more important job in this country. (Except maybe children's book author. Haha!)

*7. Some teachers are hesitant to talk about diversity with young children. What words of encouragement can you offer them?*

Be humble. Bring in diverse books, and facilitate discussion. We don't have to be the experts. We just have to model equity and intellectual curiosity.

## REFERENCES

Bennett, S. V., Gunn, A. A., Gayle-Evans, G., Barrera IV, E. S., & Leung, C. B. (2018). Culturally responsive literacy practices in an early childhood community. *Early Childhood Education Journal, 46*(2), 241–248.

Brillante, P., & Mankiw, S. (2015). A sense of place: Human geography in the early childhood classroom. *YC: Young Children, 70*(3), 6–9.

Children's Bureau. (n.d.). Retrieved from www.all4kids.org/contact-us

"Community." (n.d.). Cambridge English Dictionary. Retrieved from http://dictionary.cambridge.org/us/dictionary/english/community

Crawford, P., & Bhattacharya, S. (2014). Grand images: Exploring images of grandparents in picture books. *Journal of Research in Childhood Education, 28*(1), 128–144.

Epstein, A. S. (2009). *Me, you, us: Social-emotional learning in preschool.* Ypsilanti, MI: HighScope.

Lemieux, M. S., & Neal, J. (2010). Educating hearts: Planning for citizenship education in the primary years. *Early Childhood Education, 39*(1), 37–47.

National Association for the Education of Young Children. (n.d.). *Principles of effective family engagement.* Retrieved from www.naeyc.org/resources/topics/family-%09engagement/principles

National Council for the Social Studies. (2010). *National curriculum standards for social studies: A framework for teaching, learning, and assessment.* Silver Spring MD: Author. Retrieved from www.socialstudies.org/standards

National Council for the Social Studies. (2013). *The college, career, and civic life (C3) framework for social studies state standards: Guidance for enhancing the rigor of K–12 civics, economics, geography, and history.* Silver Spring, MD: Author. Retrieved from www.socialstudies.org/sites/default/files/2017/Jun/c3-framework-for-social-studies-rev0617.pdf

National Education Association. (2008). *An NEA policy brief: Parent, family, community involvement in education*. Washington, DC: NEA Education Policy and Practice Department. Retrieved from www.nea.org/assets/docs/PB11_ParentInvolvement08.pdf

Noddings, N. (Ed.) (2005). *Educating citizens for global awareness*. New York, NY: Teachers College Press.

Robinson, S., & Howatson-Jones, L. (2014). Children's views of older people. *Journal of Research in Childhood Education, 28*(3), 293–312.

Swick, K. J. (2004). The dynamics of families who are homeless: Implications for early childhood educators. *Childhood Education, 80*(3), 116–120.

Thompson, R. A., & Thompson, J. E. (2015). Reading minds and building relationships: This is social studies. *YC: Young Children, 70*(3), 32–39.

## Additional Children's Literature Cited

Bunting, E. (1991). *Fly away home*. Ill. by R. Himler. New York, NY: Clarion.

Bunting, E. (1997). *December*. Ill. by D. Diaz. San Diego, CA: Harcourt.

dePaola, T. (1998). *Nana upstairs and Nana downstairs*. New York, NY: Putnam.

Dooley, N. (1991). *Everybody cooks rice*. Ill. by P. Thornton. Minneapolis, MN: Carolrhoda Books/Lerner Publishing Group.

Fox, M. (1985). *Wilfrid Gordon McDonald McPartridge*. Ill. by J. Vivas. Brooklyn, NY: Kane/Miller.

Lyon, G. E. (2009). *You and me and home sweet home*. Ill. by S. Anderson. New York, NY: Atheneum Books for Young Readers.

Sis, P. (2000). *Madlenka*. New York, NY: Farrar, Straus & Giroux.

Williams, V. (1982). *A chair for my mother*. New York, NY: Greenwillow.

Wyeth, S. D. (1998). *Something beautiful*. Ill. by C. Soentpiet. New York, NY: Doubleday.

*Chapter Five*

# Partnering Globally

*Understanding the World*

- How do communities welcome outsiders, from near and far?
- What are communities like around the world? How can children benefit from learning what life is like in other contexts?
- How can global books help children to develop empathy for others, gain cultural knowledge, and build cross-cultural understanding?

This chapter focuses on stories with an international perspective and offers ideas for taking the early childhood classroom global through literature and interactive tools that can reach across borders. While best practices in early childhood education support the notion that learning should be grounded in children's life experiences, helping children engage with the world beyond their immediate surroundings is of growing importance. Case (1993) argues that exposure to knowledge about cultural differences and interconnections can help both teachers and children see intersections across local and global dimensions of our world. In addition, it is important to note that the number of immigrant and refugee families is increasing in early childhood classrooms.

According to the National Kids Count Data Center (2016), one in four children in the United States comes from an immigrant family. The families of these approximately 18 million children will be a part of our schools and communities. Stories of immigrants and refugees are especially important to consider considering the current political climate. Teachers and school leaders will need to find ways to welcome and support them; highlighting our interconnectedness, building intercultural competence, and fostering awareness are key ways to accomplish these curricular goals.

Lo and Cantrell (2002) assert that "one of the most important objectives of education for the 21st century is to foster global perspectives and global knowledge" (p. 21). They further indicate that early childhood is an ideal period for children to begin learning about international aspects in their local environment and beyond. Rosaldo (1997) coined the term *cultural citizenship* to explain the interplay between culture and citizenship. For many of the families in these books featured, their cultural background and their civic identities are the sources of conflict. Teachers can use global books as part of their toolkit as they interact with children experiencing a range of concerns from homesickness to PTSD to legal issues related to relocation.

The collection presented in this chapter is balanced to include books that celebrate cross-cultural connections as well as those that invite questions that might lead to activism. Research has shown that "teachers who understand the need for global citizens can scaffold learning to help young children become active members of a global community" (Bell et al., 2015, p. 98). Several studies in the early childhood classroom reinforce this pedagogical practice (Monobe & Son, 2014; Christie et al., 2012; Jewett, 2011; Hadaway & McKenna, 2007; Salmon et al., 2018; Martens et al., 2015; Montgomery et al., 2017). Each of these research studies involved young children moving from awareness to activism through interactions with global books.

According to Corapi and Short (2015), global literature is a "stepping stone for learning to think critically and a path to academic achievement" (p. 5). Their definition outlines three types of global literature: books that are written by immigrants to the United States and set in their home country; books written by authors who live and work across global cultures moving back and forth between the United States and their home; and books set in global cultures. The books selected for this chapter expand on those parameters with a focus on characters and topics. Lehman et al. (2010) suggest that global literature is important for fostering awareness in a range of areas including economic, environmental, world health, international immigration, and national security (p. 8). The global selections for this chapter feature immigrants and refugees to the United States as well as families living between two countries or cultures. These titles offer timely stories that reflect current events as well as universal examples of cross-cultural connections and ways to be a global citizen.

Hartung (2017) explains that global citizenship "encompasses a wide range of dimensions, from the political, moral and economic, through to the social, critical, environmental and spiritual" (p. 19). Strongly connected to this notion of global citizenship is a call for people to recognize themselves as democratic members of a global community not restricted by borders or other kinds of boundaries and barriers. Another way to think about this concept is the idea of intercultural competence.

*Intercultural competence* is defined as the ability to interact effectively with people from cultures that we recognize as being different from our own (Byram & Hu, 2017). Short et al. (2016) explore the related concept of intercultural understanding, offering three categories. These include knowledge, perspective, and action. Knowledge is based on acquiring information about global connections. Perspective involves how that knowledge is synthesized, the attitudes or explanations that result from the knowledge. The action component of intercultural understanding involves a willingness to change perspectives and more deeply consider the life experiences of others (p. 300). The importance of intercultural competence and understanding grows every day as our world becomes more global and issues of human rights cannot be avoided in the classroom.

According to the UNESCO website, global education aims to help "learners of all ages with those values, knowledge and skills that are based on and instill a respect for human rights, social justice, diversity, gender equality and environmental sustainability and that empower learners to be responsible global citizens" (UNESCO Global Citizenship Education, 2015, unpaged). Exploring global issues, even with very young children, can increase knowledge about and foster a sense of understanding toward humanity. In this way, teachers can help students develop "cosmopolitan consciousness and sense of human agency" (Choo, 2017, p. 353). The term *cosmopolitan* in this context refers to a focus on "empathy and hospitality as well as capacities to appreciate diversity and ambiguity" and "pushes for an inclusive democracy that resists the tyranny of majority values and demands attention to differences in values, perceptions, and beliefs" (p. 353). This pairing of approaches is important because teachers are often highly committed to finding ways to teach compassion, kindness, and acceptance but are not as equipped to address difference, diversity, and other tensions that may arise in order to do that work effectively.

The books selected for these text sets either take place outside of the United States or involve interactions between those in the United States and those beyond its borders. Another way to strengthen literature choices in the area of global children's literature is to select books published internationally. These books can be difficult for teachers to gain access to, but are worth the additional cost and effort. The American Library Association's Batchelder Award is a useful source for finding books that U.S. publishers have acquired and translated for American readers. Another source includes the United States Board on Books for Young People's (USBBY) Outstanding International Book List. Incorporating global perspectives in children's literature presents a unique challenge for educators at all grade levels.

Global or international children's literature rarely finds its way into teachers' hands. However, books of this nature have the potential to promote intercultural understanding by inviting children into the worlds of others.

These books expose readers to substantially different perspectives and styles than what is typically available from U.S. publishers. In addition, they offer opportunities to support National Council for the Social Studies (NCSS) standards in the areas of Culture; People, Places, and Environment; Global Connections; and Civic Ideals and Practices (www.socialstudies.org/standards/strands).

In selecting books for this chapter, several awards and lists were utilized to ensure the books were high quality, authentic, and relevant. In addition to the USBBY lists and the Batchelder Awards, the International Literacy Association's Notable Books for a Global Society (NGBS) and the National Council for the Social Studies' Notable Trade Books for Young People annual lists were consulted. The sets of books presented in this chapter and the additional recommended titles all feature contemporary issues related to global realities. Books with fantasy elements, philosophical slants, or dated storylines were eliminated. While there is value in books that romantically celebrate the joy of similarities and connectedness, such as *Whoever You Are* by Fox (1998) or *Can You Say Peace?* (Katz, 2006), the goal was to find books that invite meaningful reflection on differences while educating readers on global contexts.

As Short (2019) explains, through literature, readers "immerse themselves into story worlds" that provide experiences to move beyond "surface level tourist information to deeper cultural values and beliefs" (p. 2). Unfortunately, as Short and Acevedo (2016) discovered, early childhood educators can be hesitant to focus on intercultural learning or global education. Therefore, it is imperative for teachers to have quality resources for selecting global books and implementing approaches that explore meaningful differences, invite critical thinking, and develop compassion. Early childhood educators are witnessing in their classrooms the fact that "the everyday lives of children are no longer limited to traditional national borders" (Lehman et al., 2010, p. 8). In the following vignette, Mrs. H., a first grade teacher, used *Dear Primo*, written and illustrated by Duncan Tonatiuh (2010), to bring questions of understanding across borders to the forefront of the classroom.

## CLASSROOM VIGNETTE: *DEAR PRIMO: A LETTER TO MY COUSIN*

> My students immediately noticed the illustrations. During their picture walk, they noticed Charlie's body language and the way he was bent over, writing, on the title page and then leaping into the air on the next page. They liked guessing his emotions while going through their picture walk. They were drawn to the font that Charlie used, and we had a side conversation about typewriters, as some children knew exactly what they were, and others had no clue. It took a few pages, but they soon realized that the artwork was created

with cut-outs of different pictures of various textures and objects. Once they figured this out, they enjoyed pointing out the real-life textures they saw on the pages and choosing which ones spoke to them the most.

Two of my students speak Spanish, so they already knew the Spanish words on the pages. However, the rest of the class enjoyed using context clues to figure out what the words meant and learning some new Spanish words. The two students who speak Spanish enjoyed teaching the class how to pronounce the words correctly. Throughout the book, we would put ourselves in Carlitos's shoes and then in Charlie's shoes. We wondered if Carlitos knew what American cities were like or if Charlie knew what it was like to ride his bicycle to school every morning. We soon concluded that even if they didn't know, words are powerful and these letters that they were writing to each other really helped the cousins to understand each other's worlds in a way that they otherwise wouldn't. Some of the things that Charlie talked about, like the subway, were unfamiliar to my students. This led them to the realization that the boys' letters can help them understand both worlds as well, and that the United States is big and diverse enough that we still have much to learn about our own country.

For each theme, the students liked noticing what the cousins did and contrasting this with what they do. For example, when the boys talk about what they often eat, the students noted what they knew about what the boys ate and then talked about their own favorite foods. We also took the chance to compare and contrast Charlie's and Carlitos's worlds as we went along. They especially enjoyed this interaction with the spread where Carlitos and Charlie compare how they get their food. Some of the elements of how Carlitos obtained his food, in the open-air market, they didn't understand. I was able to share my experience from open-air markets in Ghana to help them understand a little bit more, and later we conducted research together to learn more about open-air markets that are specifically in Mexico.

When Carlitos talked about celebrating *Día de los Muertos*, most of my students made the connection to the movie Coco. I had never seen the movie, so I asked the children to compare and contrast the movie to what Carlitos probably experienced in real life. Their responses were quite extensive! When we finished the book, my class made the following conclusions: Carlitos and Charlie are not the exact same people and they do not live in the exact same place, but they can still be friends and love each other. They can visit each other and learn from each other. I affirmed these notions, and I encouraged them to look around at the people in their lives. No two people are the same, and the differences between them can help each other learn and grow. Differences and uniqueness are to be celebrated, and they are great opportunities for us.

Mrs. H. also provided some ideas to extend the selection with students.

I told the children that when I lived in Ghana, I learned exactly what they learned from this book—people who were different from me gave me a powerful opportunity to learn and make new connections. We did an exercise where every child thought of someone in their lives to share information about with the rest of the class. They had to tell how that person was different from themselves, and then why their relationship was a fantastic one.

For example, one student selected her neighbor from South Korea, while she is half Venezuelan and half American. They have different favorite colors, and they wear different clothes. My student said that she has three sisters and two brothers, while her neighbor has one brother and one sister. She said that even though they are different, they are best friends. They make each other smile and laugh. They like to sing songs for the other neighbors so they can earn money for the poor. Her neighbor taught her new foods to eat that she really likes, like kimchi.

After they finished sharing and reflecting for this exercise, I told them more about Ghana. We talked about what it was like to live there every day—what kinds of food they eat, what school is like, and what their houses are like. I then assigned each of my current students one of my former students in Ghana. They each received the child's picture, and I explained the life and personality of each child to them individually. They used a Venn diagram, as shown in figure 5.1, to compare and contrast their lives to their Ghanaian friends' lives using words and pictures. When everyone was finished, they shared their Venn diagrams with the rest of the class.

## MULTIMODAL TEXT SETS

### Text Set 1: Global Perspectives: Family and Friendship around the World

The books in this set focus on connections and aspects of culture that unify people. The stories capture the ways life is similar rather than different around the world. Children will be curious about the people they get to know

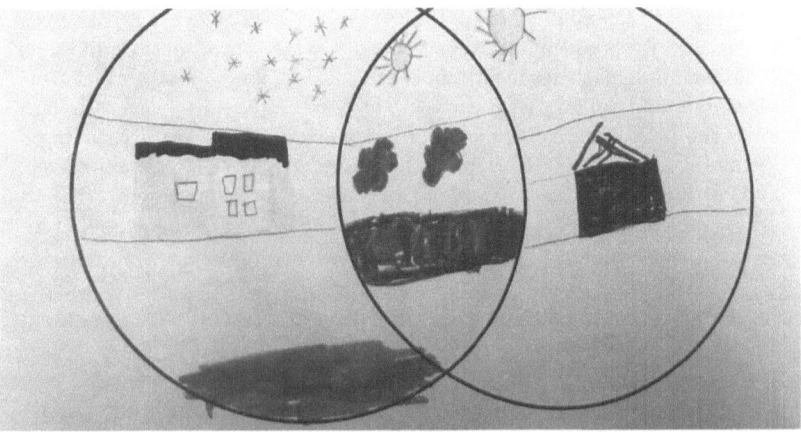

**Figure 5.1. Venn Diagram**

in these books and may ask further questions about the ways families and children live in different contexts.

Tonatiuh, D. (2010). *Dear Primo: A Letter to My Cousin.* New York, NY: Abrams Books for Young Readers.

Charlie lives in America and his cousin Carlitos lives in Mexico. Though they have never met, they exchange letters about their daily routines and interests. For example, Carlitos likes to play *fútbol* at recess while Charlie plays basketball with his friends. Despite the distance, the cousins discover that they share many similarities. With Tonatiuh's distinctive artistic style drawn from Mixtec codex, this realistic fiction selection not only received the Pura Belpré Honor Book for Illustration but also intersperses Spanish words throughout the text with a glossary. Tonatiuh also includes an author's note about his personal inspiration about writing this story.

Ajmera, M., Derstine, E. H., & Pon, C. (2014). *Music Everywhere!* Watertown, MA: Charlesbridge.

In this "Global Fund for Children" publication, this nonfiction selection provides readers with an engaging photo essay featuring over thirty countries celebrating music around the globe. The photographs range from young violinists to children singing in a gospel choir. The detailed captions and brief text showcase the inclusivity and universality of music around the world. The extensive back matter includes a world map, instructions for creating homemade instruments, and a glossary of terms. This beautiful selection will undoubtedly spark curiosity about music and culture around the world.

Kerley, B. (2009). *One World, One Day.* Washington, DC: National Geographic Society.

Told through sparse text and beautiful photographs, this selection affords readers an opportunity to explore different cultures of children around the world. Readers will note the many different ways that children around the world share similarities such as eating breakfast, going to school, and spending time with family. An author's note provides further context for the author's inspiration to create this nonfiction selection, and the world map in the back provides reference to the photographs featured.

**Text Set 1: Multimodal Activities and Extensions**

The books in this text provide readers with opportunities to learn about different cultures and geographic locations around the world. The selections support answers to questions such as: How do different groups of people living in one place influence a culture? or How can maps help us detail the journey of people, goods, or ideas around the world? Students will broaden their sense of global awareness while discussing the commonalities to their daily lives. Teachers can use Google Earth Education (www.google.com/earth/education) to locate and virtually visit different locations mentioned in the selections. If schools have access to Google Expeditions kits (https://edu.google.com/products/vr-ar/expeditions/?modal_active=none), teachers can incorporate virtual field trips to explore the different locations mentioned in *One World, One Day* (2009). As students discuss the different activities that children in other countries do during a typical school day, teachers can record their observations on an anchor chart, which can later be used for writing extensions.

Teachers can share the following video of Duncan Tonatiuh reading aloud his award-winning selection *Dear Primo* (2010) during one of his school visits: www.youtube.com/watch?v=i07FtbVLw-Q (start at 15:20). A first grade teacher, Veronica O'Leary, field-tested this selection with her students. Before reading, she passed around old letters and postcards that she has received from family and friends. She explained that the correspondence helps her to learn more about people that she cares about. By asking questions such as, "How many of you have siblings or cousins that live somewhere else from you? Have you ever received something in the mail? What did it feel like to get a card, postcard, or picture in the mail?" she provided students with opportunities to learn about the two *primos* (cousins), who are similar and different.

Since the text also includes words written in Spanish and that are labeled in the picture, Ms. O'Leary invited her class to consider: "Why are the words in Spanish written in italics? Why did the author choose that text feature to support our understanding of the Spanish words? Why are the illustrations labeled with the Spanish words? Why did the author choose this text feature to support our understanding?" Teachers can extend the opportunity for their class to learn Spanish phrases through websites such as Spanish Playground (www.spanishplayground.net/spanish-videos-kids).

Teachers can use Nearpod (https://nearpod.com) to record students' responses to questions such as: How are the cousins' interests and traditions the same and different? Describe how the environments Charlie and Carlitos live in are the same and different. Describe how the ways Charlie and Carlitos get to school are different and the same. Describe how the games Charlie and Carlitos play are the same and different. Describe how the food Charlie and Carlitos eat are the same and different, and so on. After reading the story, students can write letters to a pen pal using online pen pal programs such as www.penpalschools.com or http://members.ozemail.com.au/~penpals.

After reading *Music Everywhere!* (2014), teachers can work with their building music teacher to infuse music and instruments from around the globe. There are also some wonderful websites to with lesson ideas and music to share with students.

- Smithsonian Folkways Recordings: https://folkways.si.edu/folkways-recordings/smithsonian
- AccuRadio—World Music: www.accuradio.com/world-music
- All around This World: www.allaroundthisworld.com

**Text Set 2: Times of Crisis—Boundaries and Borders**

The focus in the books in this set is on the challenges facing children who are refugees or immigrants. All of the books have a contemporary context and share honest but hopeful stories of families experiencing displacement. While some children may have very little knowledge of current political conflicts, these books present the concepts in a simple and forthcoming way that will be engaging to young readers.

Del Rizzo, S. (2017). *My Beautiful Birds*. Toronto, ON: Pajama Press.

Sharing the perspective of a young boy named Sami, this book tells the story of a refugee child as he travels with his family and begins to settle in at a camp. Instead of focusing on his own trauma, Sami is worried about his pet pigeons. He wonders if they have escaped the war as well. The plot of the story is told partly through the selected color palette and medium. The art is created using clay and mixed media, which allows for texture and richness to permeate each page. The colors are drenched and range from soft yellows and pinks to vibrant purples and dark black. Sami finds hope as he makes new friends and new connections with nature, but ultimately this story will lead to more questions than answers for young readers.

Davies, N. (2018). *The Day War Came*. Ill. by R. Cobb. Somerville, MA: Candlewick Press.

The child-like art in this book done in pencil, colored pencil, and watercolor adds a sense of simplicity and innocence to the harshness of the story itself. The protagonist describes what happened while sitting at her desk at school: "At first, just like a spattering of hail, voice of thunder. . . . Then all smoke and fire and noise that I didn't understand." The text is straightforward and poetic with short stanzas on each page. The pictures show the desperation of this refugee child's experience as she travels alone encountering dangers and being denied even a chair to sit in so she can attend school. The book was inspired by a true story the author heard and was originally published in the *Guardian* newspaper. Responses to the story resulted in the #3000chairs movement. The voice of the child in *The Day War Came* has the potential to outrage and inspire readers of all ages.

Meddour, W. (2019). *Lubna and Pebble*. Ill. by D. Egneus. New York, NY: Dial Books for Young Readers

This book does not provide an explanation for why this family has been dislocated, but Lubna and her father find themselves in a "World of Tents." Upon arrival, Lubna finds a pebble and decides it's her best friend. She draws a face on Pebble and relies on it as a source of comfort and company. Blues, grays, and purples dominate the illustrations and capture the joy and sadness of life as a refugee. The use of perspective makes the art particularly effective. Lubna's father is positioned as larger-than-life as he embraces and watches over his child. On the final page, Amir's face stretches across the two full pages as he takes over ownership of the pebble with sad and curious eyes. Lubna's story maintains a child-centered focus while honestly portraying life in the refugee camp and during times of forced transitions.

**Text Set 2: Multimodal Activities and Extensions**

In a study conducted by Montgomery et al. (2017), children's literature about human rights was used to promote critical thinking, writing, and drawing. According to the researchers and teachers, "the students, through their drawings and interview responses, demonstrated a sense of care and empathy being at the root of their efforts to promote educational equity outside of their own classroom" (p. 13). This arts-based service-learning project in a kindergarten class can be adapted around the themes in the books in this text set.

Classroom teachers can partner with the art education specialist to help students express their thoughts and opinions in the form of protest banners and posters. The availability of a range of tools and techniques is key to the success of this project. Children can use collage, screen printing, and other forms of relief art to create words and images related to what they read about in the books.

Another way to help make the current context of the global issues in these books more accessible to young children is to focus on terminology that may be confusing or that will be empowering for them to understand. For instance, terms such as *asylum seekers*, *returnees*, and *stateless people* might need to be defined and explained in addition to the more common words such as *refugees* and *migrants*. The U.S. branch of the United Nations Refugee Agency provides engaging and accurate information for young people on this topic. They have short animated videos to explain the concepts (www.unhcr.org/en-us/teaching-about-refugees.html). Most videos are accompanied by information sheets and teaching guides as part of their "words matter" curriculum. After viewing the short animations, children could make their own versions or create responses using similar video techniques with tools such as Powtoon (www.powtown.com) or Make Belief Comix (www.makebeliefscomix.com).

In 2019, the UK hosted "refugee week" with the theme "You, me or those who came before." This theme could be adapted to a classroom context for an expanded unit. The unit can be designed around the seven simple acts featured on https://refugeeweek.org.uk/simple-acts, which include share a story, share a dish, feel the beat, and find one fact. Finding facts would pair particularly well with the books in this set, as students could search for connections and details related to the stories in books like *The Day War Came* and *My Beautiful Birds*. For instance, according to the G20 Research Group (2018), "70 million children aged zero to six years old have spent their entire lives in conflict zones." This fact could then be expanded for cross-curricular connections. How can teachers help children grasp 70 million as a number? What are some other facts about six-year-olds? How would we define a conflict zone? In this way, teachers can model and guide students as critical thinkers and researchers.

**Text Set 3: Making Connections in New Contexts**

These books feature children from families who are making their way and adjusting to life in a new context. The stories emphasize friends and family as a source of strength and support. School and home life are explored as the young protagonists navigate being true to their identities while embracing aspects of the culture or context they are joining.

Mendez, Y. S. (2019). *Where Are You From?* Ill. by J. Kim. New York, NY: HarperCollins Publishers.

This book begins with a child experiencing tension as she is repeatedly asked by her peers, "Where are you from?" She offers the answer, "I'm from here, from today, same as everyone else," but they insist, "No, where are you really from?" A double-paged spread shows the girl on one side and six questioners facing her on the opposite page. The child decides to ask her *abuelo*, who "knows everything" and also "looks like he doesn't belong." Abuelo's answer unfolds throughout the rest of the pages of the book as he reminds the girl of the beauty of her heritage, the lessons of history, and her connection to family. The illustrations, rendered in watercolor then digitally designed, conjure the natural world and invoke a celebratory mood.

Khan, R. (2010). *Big Red Lollipop*. Ill. by S. Blackall. New York, NY: Viking.

This beautifully illustrated story about sisters presents universal relationship conflicts among siblings. When Rubina, the story's oldest sibling, returns home from school with a birthday party invitation, her mother will not allow her to attend unless her middle sister, Sana, accompanies her. Unfortunately, Sana disrupts the party games and eats both her own and Rubina's big red lollipop party favors. As the years pass, it is now Sana who receives a birthday party invitation, and her mother explains that she needs to take the youngest sister, Maryam, to the party. But Rubina intervenes and persuades her mother to reconsider. In recognition of Sana's gratitude, she brings her big sister a big "green" lollipop from the party.

Kobald, I. (2014). *My Two Blankets*. Ill. by F. Blackwood. Boston, MA: Houghton Mifflin Harcourt.

When a young girl named Cartwheel and her aunt move to a new country to find refuge, everything is unfamiliar. Cartwheel finds comfort with her old blanket and soon meets a new friend. The young girl brings her new words for Cartwheel to learn in the shape of origami forms. With poetic text and beautifully rendered paintings, the story reminds readers that even a simple kindness can build a wonderful friendship.

O'Brien, A. S. (2015). *I'm New Here*. Watertown, MA: Charlesbridge.

O'Brien, A. S. (2018). *Someone New*. Watertown, MA: Charlesbridge.

This pair of books uses simple language and watercolor illustrations to create an accessible story about the transition of three children into a new school context. The page layouts offer ample white space, thick black lines, and some comic book features. In the first book, the new children—Maria from Guatemala, Jin from South Korea, and Fatimah from Somalia—describe their experiences and struggles in their own voices. Fatimah's story includes "I try to see patterns. I am scared I will make a mistake." The stories the children tell are reflected in the pictures and through speech bubbles that expand on the interactions. In the second book, Jesse, Jason, and Emma describe their experiences trying to connect with the new students. In one scene, Jesse wants to invite Maria to play soccer but worries that "our team is already great as it is. I don't want to mess it up." This honest approach to the interactions adds to the book's realism, highlighting the tensions and joys of creating a welcoming environment for students who are new to the country.

**Text Set 3: Multimodal Activities and Extensions**

Teaching Tolerance (www.tolerance.org) has developed lessons on immigration based on an online story titled *Julia Moves to the United States*. The lessons are designed to help children "to better understand who they are as individuals and who they are in relation to people around them." This directly connects to the stories in this set, which portray children adjusting to cultural and social differences. Students can listen to the story using Sound Cloud (www.tolerance.org/classroom-resources/texts/julia-moves-to-the-united-states) and then complete Venn diagrams comparing themselves to Julia. Students can create visual or written responses as they listen to the story and consider what it is like to be "that new kid in that new place." Wrap-up questions include: How can you find something in common with someone or someplace that is different than what you know? and How can we all work together to be part of a community and include everyone? These questions can serve as guiding goals for interactions with new peers from different backgrounds.

Another way to help students get to know and welcome new students is to become more familiar with geography and learn about the places their classmates are from. A variety of online map tools are available to help children explore the globe from their classrooms—for instance, the Barefoot World Atlas (https://apps.apple.com/us/app/barefoot-world-atlas/id489221652). Using this app, children can explore the world by spinning and zooming in on specific objects. By selecting photos or flags, they can read short descriptions or have the descriptions read to them. Teachers will want to visit author Rukhsana Khan's website (www.rukhsanakhan.com/books/bigredlollipop.html) for a myriad of extension activities related to *Big Red Lollipop* (2010) including a storytelling version of the story told by Khan (www.youtube.com/watch?v=N8UQWdhhy8s).

## ADDITIONAL RECOMMENDED BOOKS ABOUT GLOBAL CITIZENSHIP

Ajmera, M. (2015). *Global Baby Bedtimes.* Watertown, MA: Charlesbridge.
Ajmera, M. (2019). *Back to School.* Photo. by J. D. Ivanko. Watertown, MA: Charlesbridge.
Ajmera, M., Kinkade, S., & Pon, C. (2010). *Our Grandparents: A Global Album.* Watertown, MA: Charlesbridge.
Anonymous. (2007). *Global Babies.* Watertown, MA: Charlesbridge.
Baker, J. (2010). *Mirror.* Somerville, MA: Candlewick Press.
Bernhard, D. (2011). *While You Are Sleeping: A Lift-the-Flap Book of Time around the World.* Watertown, MA: Charlesbridge.
Buitrago, J. (2015). *Two White Rabbits.* Ill. by R. Yockteng. Toronto, ON: Groundwood Books.
Colato, L. R. (2010). *From North to South.* Ill. by J. Cepeda. San Francisco, CA: Children's Book Press.
Cox, J. (2010). *Carmen Learns English.* Ill. by A. Dominguez. New York, NY: Holiday House.
deArias, P. (2019). *Marwan's Journey.* Ill. by L. Borras. Hong Kong, China: Miniedition.
deRegil, T. (2019). *A New Home.* Somerville, MA: Candlewick Press.
Farish, T. *Joseph's Big Ride.* Ill. by K. Daley. Toronto, ON: Annick Press.
Foreman, M. (2015). *The Seeds of Friendship.* Somerville, MA: Candlewick Press.
Fox, M. (2018). *I'm an Immigrant Too.* Ill. by R. Ghosh. New York, NY: Beach Lane Books.
Gay, M. (2018). *Mustafa.* Toronto, ON: Groundwood Books.

Gravel, E. (2019). *What Is a Refugee?* New York, NY: Schwartz & Wade Books.
Hoffman, M. (2002). *Color of Home.* Ill. by K. Littlewood. New York, NY: Penguin.
Kerley, B. (2005). *You and Me Together: Moms, Dads, and Kids around the World.* Washington, DC: National Geographic.
Kerley, B. (2015). *With a Friend by Your Side.* Washington, DC: National Geographic.
Kheiriyeh, R. (2018). *Saffron Ice Cream.* New York, NY: Scholastic.
Kinkade, S. (2006). *My Family.* Photo. by E. Little. Watertown, MA: Charlesbridge.
Kostecki-Shaw, J. S. (2011). *Same, Same but Different.* New York, NY: Christy Ottaviano Books/Henry Holt.
Latour, F. (2018). *Auntie Luce's Talking Paintings.* Ill. by K. Daley. Toronto, ON: Groundwood Books.
Lucas, L. (2018). *Spectacularly Beautiful.* Ill. by L. Stein. Brooklyn, NY: Pow Kids Books.
Morales, Y. (2018). *Dreamers.* New York, NY: Holiday House.
Orbeck-Nilssen, C. (2017). *Vanishing Colors.* Ill. by K. Dickson. Grand Rapids, MI: Eerdman's Books for Young Readers.
Perkins, M. (2019). *Between Us and Abuela.* Ill. by S. Palacios. New York, NY: Farrrar, Straus, & Giroux.
Ringgold, F. (2016). *We Came to America.* New York, NY: Alfred A. Knopf.
Robinson, A., & Young, A. (2008). *Gervelie's Journey: A Refugee Diary.* Ill. by J. Allan. London, UK: Frances Lincoln Children's Books.
Ruurs, M. (2014). *Families around the World.* Ill. by J. R. Gordon. Toronto, ON: Kids Can Press.
Sanna, F. (2016). *The Journey.* New York, NY: Flying Eye Books.
Taylor, S. (2014). *Goal!* Photo. by C. Vilela. New York, NY: Henry Holt.
Williams, K. L., & Mohammed, K. (2007). *Four Feet Two Sandals.* Ill. by D. Chayka. Grand Rapids, MI: Eerdmans.
Williams, K. L., & Mohammed, K. (2009). *My Name Is Sangoel.* Ill. by K. Mohammed. Grand Rapids, MI: Eerdmans.
Williams, M. (2005). *Brothers in Hope.* Ill. by R. G. Christie. New York, NY: Lee & Low.

## AUTHOR/ILLUSTRATOR SPOTLIGHT: INTERVIEW WITH DUNCAN TONATIUH

Award-winning author/illustrator Duncan Tonatiuh was born in Mexico City and grew up in San Miguel de Allende. He graduated from Parsons New School for Design and Eugene Lang College in New York City. His body of work is inspired by ancient Mexican art, in particular the ancient art and scripts known as the Mixtec codex. Through his art and storytelling, he creates books that honor the past while addressing the contemporary issues affecting people of Mexican origin on both sides of the border.

His books include *The Princess and the Warrior*, *Esquivel: Space-Age Sound Artist!*, *Funny Bones*, *Separate Is Never Equal*, *Pancho Rabbit and the Coyote: A Migrant's Tale*, *Diego Rivera: His World and Ours*, and *Dear Primo: A Letter to My Cousin*. Tonatiuh's body of work has consistently been recognized with awards and distinctions, including the Pura Belpré Medal, the Américas Award, and the Tomás Rivera Mexican American Children's Book Award. Many of his selections have also received notable distinctions including the Jane Addams Children's Book Award, the NCTE Orbis Pictus Honor Book, and the Robert F. Sibert Medal. For more information about Duncan Tonatiuh's books and creative process, visit his website: www.duncantonatiuh.com/store.html.

*1. Please share your thinking about the importance of multicultural literature in the early childhood classroom.*

Multicultural literature is important at every age, but especially in early childhood. When children are young, they are like sponges that absorb everything. If they are exposed to multicultural literature early on, they will know that America and the world are diverse places. It will be normal for them to think of the world as a place where many different kinds of people exist. As they grow older, they are less likely to be scared of people that are different than them because they will already be familiar with them through books.

*2. Some multicultural books affirm and explore identity. Explain how you do this in your books.*

My books are all very different from one another, but the thing they have in common—the overarching theme—is that they are about Mexican culture and/or Mexican-American culture in some way.

I grew up in Mexico, but I came to the U.S. as a teenager. As I spent more time in the U.S., I began to miss things that were around me growing up, like the music, food, and traditions. I became interested in the art of Mexico and in issues that affect people of Mexican origin on both sides of the border.

When I began making books for young readers, I decided to make them about those subjects. As I continued doing it, I learned about the need for diversity in children's books. Of the thousands of books that are published in the U.S. each year for young readers, only a small percentage are about children of color. The books that are published do not reflect the diversity of children attending U.S. schools.

I think it is important for books to reflect the variety of children in the U.S. because when kids see themselves in books, they feel included and empowered. A clear example of this is when a group of fourth graders in an elementary school in Texas shared with me "Our Journeys," a multivoice poem they created about their own border-crossing experiences after they read my book *Pancho Rabbit and the Coyote*. Here is a link to the video: https://www.youtube.com/watch?v=aM6oQEVRyDc&feature=youtu.be. I was very moved when they shared the poem with me. I felt that my book had helped them know that their voices and experiences are important. I believe that is one of the powers of multicultural literature.

*3. Select one of your favorite books or poems, and share how you would explore it with young learners.*

I like the picture book *Just a Minute* by Yuyi Morales. It is a counting book full of repetition, and it is very engaging for young readers. I think

Latinx children in the classroom will feel empowered reading it because they are probably familiar with numbers in Spanish and with objects like piñatas that are mentioned in the book.

Non-Latinx students can learn about a culture and a language that is different than their own. The book can serve as an introduction to the Day of the Dead holiday. It can lead to an activity that is related to *el Día de los Muertos* like making papel picado, perforated paper.

*4. What advice would you give early childhood teachers as they attempt to explore concepts of identity with young children through multicultural literature?*

I think one of the challenges in exposing young readers to multicultural literature is making sure that the books are authentic. There are books out there that try to cash in on the diversity trend. Those books can often do a disservice because they reinforce stereotypes.
I think if possible, it is best to share a book by a person that belongs to that culture. If it is a Latinx book, then a book by a Latinx author or illustrator is probably going to be better and more authentic because that person has a lot of intrinsic knowledge about that culture because he or she has grown up in it.

Another advice is to use multicultural books throughout the year. Do not relegate Latinx books to Hispanic heritage month only. Educators can find ways to use multicultural books in all sorts of daily lessons like science, math, and writing. For example, if you are teaching young children about numbers, why not do it with *Just a Minute*? That way you are talking about numbers but also introducing children to different kinds of people and traditions.

*5. What classroom suggestions can you provide for teachers to select and incorporate diverse books into their curriculum?*

If an educator is interested in building a collection of books, one place where they can look for recommendations are awards. The awards that I am most familiar with are Latinx awards, like the Pure Belpré, the Tomás Rivera, and the Américas Award. Books that have received these awards or an honorable mention from them are chosen by librarians, teachers, professors, and other experts in the field. The selecting committees judge the quality of the writing and illustrations but often consider whether a book is authentic, and whether it has a good educational component.

The Américas Award has many educator guides for books they have awarded and honored over the years. Here is a link to them: http://claspprograms.org/pages/detail/62/Teaching-Resources. The guides have suggestions for how teachers can use the books and create units of study around them.

The Américas also creates a list of commended titles, which offers further ideas of what books an educator could acquire.

For me, as an author and illustrator, one of the most exciting things is to see how teachers and students use my books in the classroom. With *Dear Primo*, for example, I have seen educators use it as an opportunity to write letters. Some years ago, a group of students in California even corresponded with a group of students in Mexico.

*6. What are your hopes and dreams for early childhood classrooms and libraries in the future?*

More diverse books need to be published, but more diverse books need to be bought and asked for. Everyone, whether we are publishers, authors, or readers, can do our part to foster multicultural literature. I want to see libraries that display a wide variety of races, ethnicities, languages, religions, sexual orientations, and physical abilities. I think books can address all sorts of topics, even difficult or taboo ones. The challenge for creators is doing it in a way that is engaging and that students can relate to.

As the amount of diverse books increases, so will the quality and variety within each category. Latinx, for instance, are not a monolithic group. There are very many different kinds of Latinx and experiences. There are Latinx who have roots in Mexico, but there are Latinx who have roots in the Caribbean, in Central and South America. There are Latinx of different sexual orientations and Latinx of different social classes and religions. There are Latinx of mixed backgrounds. There are recent arrivals and Latinx whose families were in America before it was the U.S. In the future, I hope to see libraries that showcase a large variety of cultures but that also display the rich variety within each group.

*7. Some teachers are hesitant to talk about diversity with young children. What words of encouragement can you offer them?*

I do not think there is anything to be afraid of. Engaging with multicultural literature can be an opportunity to learn. It will require preparation and research to become familiar with a culture that is different than one's own. But if one does so in a thoughtful and respectful way, it can be a powerful opportunity for both the teacher and students to learn.

It can also be a powerful way to engage with one's students and their parents. For instance, if an educator has a large Latinx population in his or her classroom by using Latinx books and creating projects around them, the students and their parents will feel welcomed. It can be an opportunity to involve them and have them share their knowledge and expertise.

I think that sometimes people in the U.S., especially minorities, feel they need to assimilate and adopt the mainstream, predominantly white culture. But I believe that one can be a good member of the United States—be involved in one's school and in one's community—and still be proud of one's roots. I don't think those things are mutually exclusive, quite the opposite. I think that the diversity of people in this country is one of the most special and American things about the U.S.

## REFERENCES

Bell, D., Jean-Sigur, R. E., & Kim, Y. A. (2015). Going global in early childhood education *Childhood Education, 91*(2), 90–100.

Byram, M., & Hu, A. (2017). *Routledge encyclopedia of language teaching and learning.* London, UK: Taylor & Francis.

Case, R. (1993). Key elements of a global perspective. *Social Education, 57*(6), 318–325.

Choo, S. S. (2017). Globalizing literature pedagogy: Applying cosmopolitan ethical criticism to the teaching of literature. *Harvard Educational Review, 87*(3), 335–356.

Christie, E. M., Montgomery, S. E., & Staudt, J. (2012). Little by little: Global citizenship through local action inspired by Wangari Maathai. *Social Studies and the Young Learner, 25*(2), 8–11.

Corapi, S., & Short, K. G. (2015, November 30). *Exploring international and intercultural understanding through global literature.* Longview Foundation: Worlds of Words. Retrieved from https://wowlit.org/links/exploring-international-intercultural-understanding-global-literature

G20 Research Group. (2018). G20 initiative for early childhood development. Retrieved from www.g20.utoronto.ca/2018/g20_initiative_for_early_childhood_development.pdf

Hadaway, N., & McKenna, M. (2007). *Breaking boundaries with global literature: Celebrating diversity in K–12 classrooms.* Newark, DE: International Reading Association.

Hartung, C. (2017). Global citizenship incorporated: competing responsibilities in the education of global citizens. *Discourse: Studies in the Cultural Politics of Education, 38*(1), 16–29.

Jewett, P. (2011). "Some people do things different from us": Exploring personal and global cultures in a first grade classroom. *The Journal of Children's Literature, 37*(1), 20–29.

Lehman, B., Freeman, E. B., & Scharere, P. L. (2010). *Reading globally, K–8.* Thousand Oaks, CA: Corwin Press.

Lo, D. E., & Cantrell, R. J. (2002). Global perspectives for young readers. *Childhood Education, 79*(1), 21–25.

Martens, P., Martens, R., Doyle, M. H., Loomis, J., Fuhrman, L., Furnari, C., Soper, E., & Stout, R. (2015). Building intercultural understandings through global literature. *The Reading Teacher, 68*(8), 609–617.

Monobe, G., & Son, E. H. (2014). Using children's literature and drama to explore children's lives in the context of global conflicts. *Social Studies, 105*(2), 69–74.

Montgomery, S., Miller, W., Foss, P., Tallakson, D., & Howard, M. (2017). Banners for books: "mighty-hearted" kindergartners take action through arts-based service learning. *Early Childhood Education Journal, 45*(1), 1–14

National Kids Count Data Center. (2016). *Statistical snapshot: Kids in immigrant families in America today.* The Annie Casey E. Foundation. Retrieved from www.aecf.org/blog/statistical-snapshot-kids-in-immigrant-families-in-america-today

National Council of the Social Studies. (n.d.). *National Curriculum Standards for Social Studies: Chapter 2—The Themes of Social Studies.* Retrieved from www.socialstudies.org/standards/strands

Rosaldo, R. (1997). Cultural citizenship inequality, and multiculturalism. In W. Flores & R. Benmayor (Eds.), *Latino cultural citizenship* (pp. 27–38). Boston, MA: Beacon Press.

Salmon, A. K., Gangotena, M. V., & Melliou, K. (2018). Becoming globally competent citizens: A learning journey of two classrooms in an interconnected world. *Early Childhood Education Journal, 46*(3), 301–312.

Short, K. G. (2019). The dangers of reading globally. *Bookbird: A Journal of International Children's Literature, 57*(2), 1–11.
Short, K. G., & Acevedo, M. V. (2016). Creating global understandings through play. In R. Myer & K. Whitmore (Eds.), *Reclaiming early childhood literacies* (pp. 165–169). New York, NY: Routledge.
Short, K. G., Day, D., & Schroeder, J. (2016). *Teaching globally: Reading the world through literature*. Portland, ME: Stenhouse.
UNESCO Global Citizenship Education (GCED). (2015). *Global citizenship education: Preparing learning for the challenges of the twenty-first century.* Retrieved from https://unesdoc.unesco.org/ark:/48223/pf0000227729

## Additional Children's Literature Cited

Fox, M. (1998). *Whoever you are*. Ill. by L. Straub. Boston, MA: Houghton Mifflin Harcourt.
Katz, K. (2006). *Can you say peace*? New York, NY: Henry Holt.
Tonatiuh, D. (2010). *Dear primo: A letter to my cousin*. New York, NY: Abrams Books for Young Readers.

# Appendix

*Resources to Locate Diverse Selections*

### PROFESSIONAL AWARDS AND DISTINCTIONS

The American Indian Youth Award: https://ailanet.org/activities/american-indian-youth-literature-award

Américas Book Award: http://claspprograms.org/americasaward

Arab American Book Award: www.arabamericanmuseum.org/bookaward

Asian/Pacific American Award for Literature: www.apalaweb.org/awards/literature-awards

Carter G. Woodson Book Award: www.socialstudies.org/awards/woodson

Children's Africana Book Award: http://africaaccessreview.org/childrens-africana-book-awards/about-caba

Coretta Scott King Book Award: www.ala.org/rt/emiert/cskbookawards

Ezra Jack Keats Award: www.ezra-jack-keats.org/section/ezra-jack-keats-book-awards

Jane Addams Children's Book Award: www.janeaddamschildrensbookaward.org

Middle East Book Award: www.meoc.us/book-awards.html

Notable Books for a Global Society: www.clrsig.org/notable-books-for-a-global-society-nbgs.html

Pura Belpré Award: www.ala.org/alsc/awardsgrants/bookmedia/belpremedal

Rise: A feminist book list: https://ameliabloomer.wordpress.com/

Schneider Family Book Award: www.ala.org/awardsgrants/schneider-family-book-award

Stonewall Book Award: www.ala.org/rt/glbtrt/award/stonewall

Sydney Taylor Book Award: https://jewishlibraries.org/content.php?page=Sydney_Taylor_Book_Award

Tomás Rivera Book Award: www.education.txstate.edu/ci/riverabookaward

United States Board on Books for Young People (USBBY) Outstanding International Books: www.usbby.org/outstanding-international-books-list.html

## WEB RESOURCES AND BLOGS

Africa Access Review: http://africaaccessreview.org

American Indians in Children's Literature: https://americanindiansinchildrensliterature.blogspot.com

The Brown Bookshelf: https://thebrownbookshelf.com

Cooperative Children's Book Center: http://ccbc.education.wisc.edu/books/multicultural.asp

Cynthia Leitich Smith's Blog: https://cynthialeitichsmith.com

Latinx in Kid Lit: https://latinosinkidlit.com

The Open Book Blog: https://blog.leeandlow.com

Social Justice Books: A Teaching for Change Project: https://socialjusticebooks.org

We Need Diverse Books: https://diversebooks.org

# Index

adoptive/foster families. *See* family structures
Américas Award, 92, 94, 99
*And Tango Makes Three* (Richardson and Parnell/Cole), 23
*Apple Pie Fourth of July* (Wong/Chodos-Irving), 10–11, 14–15. *See also* Wong, Janet
author interviews, 14–16, 39–40, 55–57, 75–77, 92–96

*Baby's First Words* (Engel), 22
Barnes, Derrick, 55–57
Batchelder Award, 81, 82
Belpré Medal, 75, 85, 92, 94, 99
bias, xii, xvii, 2, 12, 19–20, 21, 46
*Big Red Lollipop* (Khan/Blackall), 89–90, 91
bilingual books, 11, 15, 93–94
*Black Is Brown Is Tan* (Adoff/McCully), 8
*Black White Just Right* (Davol/Trivas), 8
*Blacker the Berry* (Thomas/Cooper), 8, 9–10
book awards, for diverse literature, xviii, 14, 39, 55, 81, 82, 92, 94, 99–100
book discussions. *See* classroom vignettes
books as mirrors, xii, xiv–xv, xviii, 1, 4–5, 21, 39, 55–56
Brown, Monica, 5, 11, 12
bullying, 24, 44, 45–46, 53–54

Caldecott Medal, 4, 43, 55, 63, 67
*Can I Touch Your Hair?* (Latham and Waters/Qualls and Aldo), 11, 12
*A Chair for My Mother* (Williams), 63
*Chrysanthemum* (Henkes), 44
citizenship, fostering, 59–60, 61–62, 69–71, 80–81
classroom expectations, 51–52
classroom vignettes, 5–8, 25–29, 47–49, 63–66, 82–84
Common Core standards, 14
communities, local: celebrating, 59, 61, 72–74; defining, 60; fostering connections to, xvii, 59–60, 61–62, 64–66, 73–74; geography of, 61, 73; diverse members of, 60, 61, 62, 68–69, 73; poverty in, 63–64, 69–71; problems in, 62–63, 69–71; teaching about, 59, 61–63, 66, 68–69, 70–71, 73–74
Cooperative Children's Book Center, xiv, 56, 100
critical thinking, promoting, 5, 7–8, 47, 59, 63, 82, 88–89
cross-cultural connections, xi, 80, 82–87, 91, 93, 95–96
cultural authenticity, xii, 3, 5, 29, 82, 94
cultural identity. *See* identity, cultural/ethnic
cultural citizenship. *See* citizenship, fostering
cultural pride, 1, 5, 95–96

cultural understanding, promoting, 5, 11–12, 61, 90–91
culturally responsive teaching, xii

*Daniel's Good Day* (Archer), 72
*The Day War Came* (Davies/Cobb), 87–88, 89
*The Day You Begin* (Woodson/López), 51
*Dear Primo: A Letter to My Cousin* (Tonatiuh), 82–84, 85, 86, 92. *See also* Tonatiuh, Duncan
de la Peña, Matt, 64, 69, 75–77
difference: awareness of, 4–5, 7, 20, 46; and friendships, 43–44; respect for, 1, 10–11, 40, 83, 85–86; starting conversations about, xi, xii, 3, 4, 5, 6–7, 12, 20. *See also* racial/ethnic awareness among young children
digital/online resources for diversity: art resources, 10, 73; Creative Commons, 12; Family Diversity Project, 34; family tree tools, 29, 35; kindness resources, 51–52, 54; language resources, 86; mapping tools, 73–74, 86, 91; memorial and memory box tools, 37–38, 68; music resources, 87; podcasts, 52; recording tools, 7, 37, 54, 68, 86; scrapbooking tools, 9; story writing tools, 9, 34, 38, 68–69; SoundCloud, 15, 91; Teaching Tolerance resources, 10, 28, 35, 90–91; video resources, 9–10, 12, 32, 34, 54, 71, 86, 88–89; websites, 100; word cloud tools, 9–10, 54
diverse children's literature: importance in the classroom, xi–xv; selecting, xi, xviii, 3, 5, 8, 20, 21–22, 44, 49, 60–61, 63, 80, 94–95; supplemental lists, 12–14, 38–39, 55, 74–75, 91–92. *See also* multimodal resources and extension activities for diversity; poetry collections; text sets for diversity
*Donovan's Big Day* (Newman/Dutton), 36
*Drawn Together* (Le/Santat), 67

*Each Kindness* (Woodson/Lewis), 47–48, 53, 76
early childhood curriculum, xi, 2, 3, 15, 20, 79; anti-bias curriculum, 2, 3, 31; designing lessons for, 3, 20; languages in, 14, 15, 83, 94; poetry, incorporating, 16, 38, 93; role of literature in, 3, 4, 5, 7; standards for, xi, 20. *See also* National Association for the Education of Young Children standards
elderly, children's connections to, 62
empathy. *See* kindness and empathy
ethnic identity. *See* identity, cultural/ethnic
*Everybody Cooks Rice* (Dooley/Thornton), 61

families: activities related to, 20, 28–29, 31–32, 34–35, 37–38; affirmation of different types, 20, 29, 32–34; and children's development, xvi–xvii, 19; demographics, in United States, 19–20, 21, 22, 24; portrayed in children's literature, 19, 20–25, 29–34; promoting conversations about, xvii, 19, 27–28, 31–32, 35; sibling relationships within, 21, 33; teacher support for, 37–38, 59; trauma/loss within, 21, 24–25, 30, 32, 35–36
*Families Families Families* (Lang and Lang), 20
*A Family Is a Family Is a Family* (O'Leary/Leng), 25–29, 31
*The Family Book* (Parr), 20
family diversity. *See* family structures
family-school connections, 19, 68
family structures, xvi–xvii, 19–21; adoptive/foster, 19, 21, 23, 25, 27, 30, 37; blended/step, 19; divorced, 19, 21, 30, 32; immigrant/refugee, 79, 87–88, 89–90; interracial/multiracial, 19, 21, 22, 30, 33; LGBTQ, 19, 21, 23, 31, 34, 39; multigenerational, 21, 28; single-parent, 19, 21, 22, 24, 33; two-parent/traditional, 19, 21, 25
family tree activities, 28–29, 35
first day of school, 44, 50–51, 90
Fred Rogers Center, 74
*Fred Stays with Me* (Coffelt/Tusa), 30, 31
friendships at school: and conflict resolution, 43, 44, 53–54; cross-cultural/cross-race, 44, 45, 46–47, 84–85, 90; cultivating and navigating, xvii, 43, 44–46, 52–54; defining, 44,

46; and social development, 45; starting conversations about, 43, 45, 48, 54; teacher support for, 45–47, 51–52, 57

gender, discussion of, 5, 39. *See also* identity
gender-exclusive events, 20
global citizenship. *See* citizenship, fostering
global perspectives: and activism, 80, 88–89; geography instruction and, 85, 91; starting conversations about, 82–84; teaching, xvii–xviii, 79–80, 81–84, 85–87. *See also* immigrants and refugees; intercultural competence
graffiti board, 7
grandparents, 21, 28, 66–68. *See also* elderly; family structures
grief, support for, 24–25, 37–38

Habitat for Humanity, 64, 71
*Hair Dance!* (Johnson/Johnson), 8–9
*Hair Love* (Cherry/Harrison), 11, 12
*Happy In Our Skin* (Manushkin/Tobia), 9–10
*Heather Has Two Mommies* (Newman), 23. *See also* Newman, Leslea
homelessness, 21, 62–63, 71
homophobia. *See* bias
*Hooway for Wodney Wat* (Lester/Munsinger), 44

*I Walk with Vanessa* (Kerascoët), 53
identity: activities related to, 9–10, 11–12, 15–16; affirming, xvi, 1–2, 3, 4–5, 7, 24, 39, 55–56, 76; challenges to, 10–11; cultural/ethnic, 1, 2, 4–5; development of, xiii, xvi, 1, 2, 4–5, 76–77; multiracial, 11, 21–22; racial and cultural dimensions of, 1, 4–5; impact of educators on, 2, 4, 5, 11–12, 23–24
identity markers, 1, 3
*I'm New Here* (O'Brien), 90
immigrants and refugees, 79–80, 87–89; supporting, 79, 89; teaching about, 88–89, 90–91
incarceration of parent. *See* families, trauma/loss within
inclusion, 15, 34–35, 45

intercultural competence, xii, 79, 80–81
international perspectives. *See* global perspectives; immigrants and refugees
intersectionality, 2, 21, 23

*Julián Is a Mermaid* (Love), 67
*Just a Minute* (Morales), 93–94

Keats, Ezra Jack. *See The Snowy Day*
kindness and empathy, fostering, xii, 47–49, 51–54, 81
*The King of Kindergarten* (Barnes/Brandley-Newton), 50, 55. *See also* Barnes, Derrick
*The Kissing Hand* (Penn), 44
*Knock Knock: My Dad's Dream for Me* (Beaty/Collier), 36

*Last Stop on Market Street* (de la Peña), 64, 69. *See also* de la Peña, Matt
Latinx book awards. *See* book awards
*Lena's Shoes Are Nervous* (Calabrese/Medina), 50
*Living with Mom and Living with Dad* (Walsh), 32
LGBTQ families. *See* family structures
*Lubna and Pebble* (Meddour/Egneus), 88

*Madlenka* (Sis), 61
*Marianthe's Story: Painted Words* (Aliki), 44
*Marisol McDonald Doesn't Match* (Brown/Palacios), 5–8, 11, 12
*Mom, It's My First Day of Kindergarten* (Yum), 50
multimodal resources and extension activities for diversity, xii; author suggestions for, 15, 40, 56, 76–77, 94; on community challenges, 70–71; on cross-cultural connections, 85–87; on family affirmation, 31–32, 34–35; on family transitions and loss, 37–38; on friendship, 54; on immigrants and refugees, 88–89, 90–91; on intergenerational connections, 68–69; on music, 86–87; on neighborhoods, 73–74; on starting school, 51–52; on self-awareness, 9–10; on self-confidence, 11–12. *See also* digital/

online resources for diversity
multiracial identity. *See* identity, multiracial
*Music Everywhere!* (Ajmera, Derstine, and Pon), 85
*My Beautiful Birds* (Del Rizzo), 87, 89
*My City* (Liu), 72–73
*My Papi Has a Motorcycle* (Quintero/Peña), 56, 73
*My Pop Pop and Me* (Smalls), 67–68
*My Town's (Extra) Ordinary People* (Casal), 72
*My Two Blankets* (Kobald/Blackwood), 90

*Nana in the City* (Castillo), 67
*Nana Upstairs and Nana Downstairs* (de Paola), 62
National Association for the Education of Young Children (NAEYC) standards, xii, xv, 2, 19, 44
National Council for the Social Studies (NCSS) standards, 61, 62, 82
National Council of Teachers of English (NCTE), 14, 75, 92
neighborhoods. *See* community, local
Newbery Medal, 75
Newman, Leslea, 39–40

*The One Day House* (Durango), 70, 71
*One World, One Day* (Kerley), 85, 86
*One Word from Sophia* (Averbeck/Ismail), 30
*Our Gracie Aunt* (Woodson/Muth), 36
*Owen* (Henkes), 44

*Pancho Rabbit and the Coyote* (Tonatiuh), 93
parents, communicating with, 19
*Paula Knows What to Do* (Dufft), 30
peer culture, 44–45, 48
persona dolls, 31
physical traits, celebrating, 1–2, 4–5; books and activities related to, 8–10
poetry collections, 8, 11, 12, 14
Poetry Friday Anthology Series, 14–15
prejudice. *See* bias

racial/ethnic awareness among young children, 1, 2–3, 4, 6; actions related to, 2–3; preferences related to, 4
racial identity. *See* identity
racial pride, 1, 3, 4–5, 6
racism. *See* bias
*Red* (deKinder/Watkinson), 53

*The Scar* (Moundlic/Tallec), 35
self-concept, developing, 2, 3
self-confidence, xviii, 1, 4, 6, 7, 10–12, 31
service-learning projects, 68, 71, 88
*Shades of People* (Rotner), 9
single-parent families. *See* family structures
*The Snowy Day* (Keats), 4
social-emotional learning, 2, 45, 61, 68
socioeconomic diversity, connecting across, 47, 60–61, 66, 69–71
*Someone New* (O'Brien), 90
*Something Beautiful* (Wyeth/Soentpiet), 60–61
*Sparkle Boy* (Newman), 40
standards, curriculum. *See* early childhood curriculum
*Star of the Week* (Friedman/Roth), 30, 31
*Stella Brings the Family* (Schiffer/Clifton-Brown), 31
stereotypes, challenging, xii, 3, 46–47, 62, 94
*Stick and Stone* (Ferry/Lichtenheld), 44
Stonewall Award, 23, 39

Teaching Tolerance resources. *See* digital/online resources for diversity
*Ten Days and Nine Nights: An Adoption Story* (Heo), 36–37
text sets for diversity: on community and socioeconomic issues, 69–70; criteria for inclusion in, xvi, 8, 21–22, 25, 44, 49, 63, 66, 80, 81–82; on family affirmation, 29–31; on family interactions, 32–34; on family transitions, 35–37; on the first day of school, 50–51, 90; on global/intercultural perspectives, 85, 89–90; on immigrants and refugees, 87–88, 89–90; on intergenerational connections, 66–68; on making friends,

52–54, 90; on personal challenges and conflicts, 10–11; on self-awareness (physical traits), 8–9; on self-confidence, 10–11; supplemental books supporting, 12–14, 38–39, 55, 74–75, 91–92. *See also* multimodal resources and extension activities
texts, constructing meaning from, 4
*Those Shoes* (Boelts), 69, 71
Tonatiuh, Duncan, 85, 86, 92–96

United States Board on Books for Young People Outstanding International Books, 81, 100

Vardell, Sylvia, 14, 15
Venn diagrams, 12, 84, 91

video resources. *See* digital/online resources for diversity
*Visiting Day* (Woodson/Ransome), 32–33

We Need Diverse Books, xiv, 40, 76, 100
*Where Are You From?* (Mendez/Kim), 89
*Whitewash* (Shange/Sporn), 8
whole child nurturing, 3, 4–5, 12
*Wilfred Gordon McDonald Partridge* (Fox/Vivas), 62
*Will I Have a Friend* (Cohen), 44
Wong, Janet, 10, 12, 14–16

*Yo? Yes!* (Raschka), 43
*You and Me and Home Sweet Home* (Lyon/Anderson), 63–66, 70, 71
YouTube videos. *See* digital/online resources for diversity

# About the Authors

**Lesley Colabucci** is an associate professor of early, middle, and exceptional education at Millersville University of Pennsylvania, where she teaches courses in children's literature at the graduate and undergraduate level.

**Mary Napoli** is an associate professor of reading at Penn State Harrisburg, where she teaches literacy education and children's literature courses at the undergraduate and graduate level.

www.ingramcontent.com/pod-product-compliance
Lightning Source LLC
Chambersburg PA
CBHW030145240426
43672CB00005B/274